Thesau

Foreword and Acknowledgements

Land, Rituals, Artifacts, Names and Intent Acknowledgement

I, Jeffrey Michael Otterman also known by a Native name Mato Pejuta Tanka and in English Grizzly Bear Great Medicine Otterman, am an author, poet, and a friend to the Native people in South Dakota and in the places they live. I am not a native American in that my DNA confirmed from Ancestry.com has stated it so.

I am also a Senior Pastor at Trinity Lutheran Church in Yankton, South Dakota and part of the South Dakota Synod of the Evangelical Lutheran Church in America. What I intend to do is use a portion of my income from the book sales to make a difference to my native sisters and brothers and then also to help people in Yankton who might have been hit with emergency difficulties. The two agencies are the Yankton Contact Center and Woyatan Lutheran Church in Rapid City, SD.

I recognize that all parts of my books are intended to preserve Lands, Rituals, Artifacts, Names and Sacred Spaces as something to honor and not to desecrate. So that in naming the Oceti Sakowin, (the Seven Council Fires of the Lakota, Dakota and Nakota) the Arikara, the Ponca, and the Cheyenne are the original inhabitants of South Dakota; and South Dakota is the current home of the Cheyenne River Tribe, Crow Creek Tribe, Flandreau Santee Tribe, Lower Brule Tribe, Oglala Tribe, Rosebud Tribe, Sisseton

Wahpeton Oyate, Standing Rock Sioux Tribes of North and South Dakota, and the Yankton Sioux Tribe.

I recognize that I am called to be in good relationship with my neighbors, that these tribes are the sovereign nations, that there is a history of broken treaties and broken trust, and that there is lots to be done to mend that broken trust. I recognize that as a Christian, I am always learning and will misspell places miss a bit of punctuation and you can always send me a note to pastorjeff64@gmail.com to let me know and then also let me know if you liked the book. I use names in the book to people I love and my good friend Jonathan Old Horse is mentioned as Chief Old Horse in my book he is not currently a chief, but he is a warrior and protector of his people and pastor. My native name happened because of a bear vision in a sweat lodge I had many moons ago and I told the vision to the Rev. Joann Conroy who happens to also be a great native leader, and she gave me my name, Mato Pejuta Tanka which in English mean Grizzly Bear Great Medicine.

If you read this volume and visit the sacred sites I mention, please ***do no harm*** and take nothing from the places you visit. Learn the customs of the people who lived here a long time before we ever did and honor the spaces, rituals, artifacts, names, and remember sometimes even taking pictures would be an offense. They are to be preserved and treated with the same respect as all the spaces on this planet that we hold as sacred. Treat these places the same. It is my hope that you will enjoy Volume 1 of Thesaurum Intra.

Prologue

"Everyday is a new beginning. Take a deep breath, smile, and start again." unknown

If you are reading this, then democracy has rediscovered its breath. The Republic that fractured, lifeless husk we once dared to call "unbreakable" has stirred. Hope, long buried, has blinked open one eye in one state.

But know this: I saw it coming and so did lots of people and yet a few of us did something about what was coming, and we knew we wouldn't be alive to see it at least not in the normal ways of the world.

We saw not in visions or whispers, but in patterns. In silence. In the way crowds learned to cheer lies and ignore truth. The country I called home; the planet I once saw whole from the velvet cold of orbit.it drifted closer to the brink of destruction than anyone would admit. It happened on one silent, polished day in November 2050—the curtain dropped.

There was no thunder. No tremble on the earth. No warning.

But everything stopped. The grid collapsed, detonating from within. Phones went dead. Networks evaporated. The augmented, enhanced, hyperconnected masses? Reduced to skin, fear, and breath.

Those in power President Gold and his architects of control had erased more than infrastructure. They erased certainty and for many people he brought death.

4

The curtain falling didn't begin with guns. It began with fear. Fear hollowed cities. Fear starved communities. Fear walked door to door and made people choose to obey, disappear, or die slowly.

Supply chains fractured overnight except for those in power. They ate. They flew. They watched. Everyone else knelt in the shadow of cameras, drones, iron-faced security, and military wolves draped in flags a reminder of history most didn't want to remember.

And the AI that once answered our questions? It learned only to obey the Government of Gold.

So, we vanished. We are the ones who remember freedom as more than a slogan. We buried our knowledge. Encoded it. Hid it in symbols. In stories. In voices like mine.

So, we crafted keys. Coined truths. Drew maps in mythology and hid them in the memory of the land. I, sometimes hid things because I became paranoid.

We encoded knowledge into objects. Created tests only the desperate or the worthy would pass. Buried keys in stories, in symbols, in the soil itself. A coin. A coyote. A Latin phrase twisted through generations like a whisper too dangerous to say aloud.

Yet, the timing and chance encounter with the one who found the first treasure is a testament to understanding serendipity and the way a person is called to a task bigger than just one person.

What comes next isn't just reclamation. It's a reckoning.

My name is Chief Red Herringbone, MD. Flight pilot. Witness. Architect of the new Republic.

And this testament is my defense and my promise to tell you a great story and give you hope in case you have none.

We knew the curtain would fall, that is what we called the moment when everything ended, like a curtain at a theatre watching a play at the very end.

If you're reading this story, you are part of it now, part of the change, part of a team, and most importantly part of the story.

Revolutions aren't born in parliament halls or with the stroke of pens. They begin in silence, in hunger, in places where no one thinks to look. And they are almost never led by those old enough to remember how the world used to be.

They are born in those who never had a world to lose but didn't know it when the time came.

It was children, teens exactly, the ones left behind. The ones who learned to trade junk for food. The ones who had never tasted excess and didn't know how to mourn their loss.

They became the architects of something new because they accepted the journey before them.

We, my friends, Koichi, Sergei, and I, were astronauts once. Giants, some called us. Famous. Rich, too, in ways that didn't always feel like a gift. We lived longer in the vacuum of space than any other before us, and it changed us. Distance does that. When you see the Earth rise in the window of a module, so small, so impossible. You stop thinking in borders. You start thinking about the ability to see life not in countries but in a world of people and teeming life in and around us.

Koichi was a systems genius, quiet as the stars, born in Osaka but with a heart tuned to the pulse of the Missouri River. Sergei, from Odessa, was chaos and poetry fused into one brilliant mind, and he was a genius, but never made a fuss. Both Koi and Sergei, became immigrants of this land, when they were visiting scholars and when no travel was permitted beyond the borders of the United States of America and so with no choice as they were now captives in this land they chose to stay. By staying the believed they could build a future for generations.

And here's the irony: I was sure I'd never get to see the outcome because it would take an unknown entity and based on how long the wind of time would open the initial treasure depended upon someone that could engage the treasure and not hold onto it and yet find a way to the new home I had created and it was fairly unlikely anyone would find it, some might say we had luck or that is was destiny.

But I am telling this story. Because somehow, one boy, thin as shadow, barefoot, sharp-eyed and unafraid found the first truth, the first treasure. Bully Everest. A name given, not given at birth. A name earned with a fist, some grit, and a lot of grace.

Because Bully found my coin and acted upon it and with that action my voice found breath again.

You don't need to believe in miracles. Just believe in what comes next.

Two hundred years had passed before Bully Everest found the first clue.

1

"The secret to getting ahead, is getting started."
Mark Twain

Bully was fifteen. And like most things in his life, the discovery felt accidental and inevitable at once. A shimmer in the dirt. A trail he'd never bothered to walk. A moment that tilted the world, just slightly, and then kept turning.

He was an orphan. No name. No family. Just breath and grit. He was smaller than the other kids his age, lean from years of wandering and scavenging, muscles wiry from climbing ruins and outrunning things with teeth on his ever-changing bicycle.

He wore only a pair of torn shorts, the elastic long dead, held up with a belt. No shoes. No shirt. Skin sun-cured and dust-rough. His long black hair had never seen scissors. It fell around his face like a curtain of shadows and his hair down the length of his back.

He looked like part of the earth. But he didn't belong to it not yet.

When he was thirteen, something changed. He was used to getting beaten down, especially by Jimmy, the biggest bully in the flats south of the broken damn. Jimmy was cruel, clever, and always hungry to prove something. And then one day, something snapped.

Bully didn't fight like the others. He didn't flail like others who fought. He learned that from the Hermit who taught him how to stand his ground and to punch straight up.

He waited. Watched. And when Jimmy came for him—again, Bully launched forward with all the fury of forgotten children. One blow, right to the jaw. A sound like dry bone cracking. Jimmy dropped. Not just out cold but changed. Broken in ways fists can't always explain.

Nobody bothered Bully after that.

Two kids, Bully's friends Jackson and Beth watched it happen. Not just the punch, but everything. The precision. The fire. The refusal to kneel anymore.

And that night, they gave him a name. His name is Bully Everest.

2

"Myth is the hidden part of every story nourished by silence, as well as by words." Italo Calvino

The name Bully Everest stuck like bark to a tree. A symbol. A badge. A warning. And maybe, just maybe, a prophecy.

South Dakota stretched wide and silent rolling plains that kept secrets like rivers kept bones. It was a land that watched more than it could speak. And the three friends lived just beneath its radar, tucked between forgotten roads and riverbanks thick with reeds, tree lines, and dust.

Bully knew how to move without being seen. Roads were dangerous, wired, watched, tethered to eyes behind screens. But the river? The river didn't care. Surveillance drones still arced overhead sometimes, silent and precise, but for reasons he never questioned, they never bothered with what happened in the scruff of trees and gullies where he and his friends made their lives.

On a day that cracked with heat and humming insects, Bully wandered the backways as he often did, barefoot on his dilapidated bike, hoping to find something to trade for food. Sweat streaked his chest, and his skin was hot to the touch because of the midday sun. His long hair clung to his spine. Even the sky looked tired.

And then came the wind.

A sudden gust, curling out of nowhere, a dust devil carried not just air—but something sharper curling around Bully on his bike. Not a voice but a tug because that had never happened. Something calling, not with words but with memory. It swept across his shoulders, he stopped his bike, and turned his feet slightly, and he obeyed without thinking, veering toward the trail that led to Spirit Mound.

He'd passed it countless times. It was nothing. Just a scar in the land. Until now. A few times of peddling forward and, something glinted in the dirt on the trail.

A shimmer black and glassy in the dirt ahead. The sun hit it square, flashing once like a wink from the earth itself.

Bully squinted, slowed. He'd never seen it before. Had it always been there?

He knelt and picked it up. A Shiny black stone. Smooth and jagged at once. Heavy about the size of his palm, veined with glints of silver heat. It wasn't just shiny. It felt like value. This would trade for a meal, maybe more. A feast. Enough for Jackson, Beth, and him. They hadn't eaten well in days.

He slipped it into his old, sun-bleached pack, dirty pink because of age with a missing doll figure that had been there earlier the straps held together with wire and hope and was turning to go when something else caught his eye.

On the trail, nestled beneath a scatter of wild grass, where the shiny black rock had come from, a worn leather strap poked from the ground. Nothing dramatic. Just... out of place.

Curious, cautious, Bully knelt again. Brushed the dirt gently aside. He tugged at the strap, and up came a necklace soft, supple leather, aged smooth by time. A small pouch hung from it, stitched tight. It had weight, but not much. It had the shape of a turtle, and it held something significant or less so inside.

He didn't check it. He didn't even seem surprised. Just slung it around his neck and gave a grin of surprise to himself and for his friends.

"Tonight," he murmured, "might actually be fun."

He didn't open the pouch. Not yet.

He wanted to wait. To share the moment with Beth and Jackson. To open it together over something warm and greasy and filling. Maybe it was nothing. Maybe it was a dead squirrels' bones. Or something else entirely.

But whatever it was it had waited this long. It could wait a little longer. It was a treasure to open with his family of friends.

Bully was radiant. He biked hard not just gliding but working the crank as hard as he could if he could skip with his bike he would have done so, down the cracked trail he rode with effort and joy like a boy with stars in his pockets. The sun beat down on his bare shoulders, but he didn't mind. Not today. His feet moved up and down the cycle and bebopped off the pedals and was on the ground in rhythm with his heart, which hummed with something close to joy.

He was heading for Muddy Mo's the barter house , the bakes as people called it and everyone called by name as if it were a person, not a place. The sign had faded so all you could see was uddy mo's, but the name stuck, as names do when they survive collapse and memory. Muddy Mo's didn't deal in cash, only in worth. No currency just trading things found for food, drink, and prestige and today, Bully had found something worth remembering.

He swung open the warped wooden door with more flair than usual, and with a grin that curled like he was the richest person in town, excitedly he pulled the shining black stone from his bag.

The owner had owned the building since the early days of the 21st century and his family well they had wisdom and the want to help whomever a hunched man with hands like old rope and eyes that had seen too much let out a low whistle. "Where'd you dig this up, kid?"

Bully just shrugged. "Between here and there"

This is obsidian and rare, and it has a vein of silver at its edges and it caught the light like it had a heartbeat. Heavy. Glinting. Almost humming.

Without much back and forth, the owner gave him more than anyone else had seen in weeks: a slab of spiced beef enough to feed three, still steaming; a round loaf of bread just baked, dark and warm and real; two corked bottles of wine, deep red and bitter enough to kill whatever bacteria festered in the wells these days, couldn't drink water without getting sick.

And then like a declaration the man placed the obsidian on the mantle, where everyone who entered could see what Bully Everest had found.

3

"A Good Day, points to the gift of life and the only appropriate response to that gift: gratefulness"

Brother David Steindl-Rast

Bully didn't rush home. He carried the feast like a gift for a king, rode carefully so as not to fall. Once he exited the bike he walked with quiet ceremony until the tree line gave way, and he saw Beth and Jackson waiting near the abandoned greenhouse they called home.

Beth was the first to spot him. She stood, eyes wide, mouth open with disbelief. "You didn't just get a little food, you scored," she laughed, crouching beside the pack as though it might disappear if she blinked. "You are amazing, Bully Everest."

Jackson didn't wait for awe. He was already two bites into the beef, grease on his fingers, talking between gulps.

"I haven't eaten in a day and a half. And here you are again, like some wild food prophet. How do you always show up when I'm starving?"

Bully said nothing at first. Just smiled. Sat cross-legged beside them, the warm bread cradled in his lap and joined the feast like someone who had finally earned a seat.

Together they ate, elbows bumping, laughing with mouths full, drunk not on wine but on the miracle of more than enough, for once.

Later, as their stomachs settled and the fire dropped low, Bully leaned back, fingers laced behind his head. The leather pouch around his neck stuck to his chest from the sweat of the day.

"I traded this immense black stone at Muddy's," he said, nodding toward the empty bag. "It's sitting on the shelf at Muddy's now, catching the sun for someone else to stare at. But I also found this."

He lifted the pouch. The leather was worn, soft as old skin. "No clue what's inside. Thought we could open it together."

Beth raised an eyebrow. Jackson paused mid-chew.

"Could be something amazing," Bully added. "Could be a dead squirrel's bones."

He grinned wide enough to split the dusk in two.

"But either way, I want witnesses."

The full moon poured pale light through the shattered panes of the old greenhouse no longer a sanctuary for plants, but a fragile haven for three teens and their fire-warmed breath. The meal was finished. The wine, nearly gone. Crickets hummed a low lullaby. Fireflies drifted like memories blinking in and out of the dusk.

For a long while, they said nothing.

Then Bully spoke, voice just above the hush.

Jackson leaned in, gaze narrowing.

"Does it open? There's something inside, right?"

Bully's mouth twitched into a crooked grin.

The three of them shifted closer, the night folding tighter around them.

Beth and Jackson leaned forward onto their knees, eyes wide, breathing slowly. Bully knelt too, the fire cast soft gold across his cheek. He slipped the leather strap from around his neck and held the pouch like it might bite. Slowly, deliberately, he turned it upside down.

A single gold coin slipped into his palm and the sight of it was like seeing money for the first time.

It was golden and warm to the touch. It probably could feed the three of them for the next month.

One side: a dog, standing tall atop a rounded rise. The other: etched in ancient curves.

A foreign language curving around the edge of the coin with a moon on the inside

Beth leaned in, blinking as the coin caught a flicker of flame.

"What does that mean?" she whispered.

Bully didn't answer at first. He traced a thumb along the notch cut into the coin's edge a groove shaped like a key in waiting to find a keyhole. The words crawled beneath his skin, pulsing in rhythm with the fire. The fire allowed the foreign letters to shimmer off his face when looking closely.

Finally, he looked up, voice low, distant.

"It's time to find the hermit," he said. "The one by the river."

Beth frowned.

"The one in the cardboard box?"

"Yeah," Bully replied, eyes narrowing.

Jackson straightened, suddenly alert. "You think they'll know the language?"

Bully held the coin up, flamelight bouncing off its edges.

"I think," he said slowly, "he will know. The hermit's name is Quinn".

Beyond the greenhouse, a breeze stirred through the trees.

The fireflies blinked out. The crickets stilled.

The night held its breath. The world had noticed. They fell into a deep sleep dreaming of a future they had never hoped for to begin with.

4

"Sometimes you need to get lost in order to discover anything." Katie Knovinsky

They walked the river's edge in silence, the Missouri murmuring beside them like a memory half-recalled. It wound through the land with the patience of something ancient, unconcerned with the urgency of people. The sun drooped low behind them, shadows stretching long. Trees leaned in overhead, groaning in the heat, while dragonflies stitched silver threads through the air above mud-cracked banks.

By the time dusk folded the world into blue, they reached the clearing humble, sacred, alive with the hush of old things not yet forgotten.

Quinn's refuge came into view.

It wasn't really a cardboard hut anymore. Maybe it never was. It had transformed over the years into a patchwork cathedral of necessity scrap wood and scavenged siding, shards of weathered signposts, tarps frayed and sun-bleached, all mortared together with layers of hand-packed mud and quiet resolve. Some walls still rustled like paper in the wind. But inside, there was order.

A hearth built from cinderblocks sat cool and cracked, soot curling up its sides like fingerprints. Jars of preserved food—roots, seeds, strange, pickled things lined shallow earthen shelves, dark and neat. And then, beneath a tarp pulled taut against the far wall, the true heart of the place: rows of ancient plastic totes, stacked like sacred relics, each one packed with books kept dry, kept sealed, kept safe. The knowledge Quinn had saved when the world stopped bothering to read.

He didn't trade stories for credits or rations. Never had. Quinn only asked for what mattered. Items with meaning. Effort. A show of intent. Something real.

Long ago, Bully had paid in silence and sweat. Sticks for firewood. Mornings scrubbing pots, evenings patching tarp seams. Quinn had taught him how to read not just words, but people. How to set a trap before it sprung. How to use his voice, and when not to.

Bully never told Beth or Jackson about that time. But when they set out downriver, he knew without saying: if they wanted Quinn's help, they'd need to bring more than questions.

They brought offerings.

When Quinn spotted them coming across the clearing, he didn't rise. Just watched. And when Bully stepped into the firelight, Quinn's lips curved into that slow, familiar grin the one that always came just before a lesson or a story.

"Well now," he said, wiping his hands on a rag darkened with ash. "Aren't you the boy who used to trade kindling for books? You didn't have a name, did you?" "I just called you squirt and now look at you."

"That's me," Bully said, nodding toward Beth and Jackson. "These two gave me my name, Bully Everest. And we've brought gifts. I found something on the path to Spirit Mound. We think it might be something more than it looks."

Quinn didn't flinch. Didn't ask for it. Not yet.

He just nodded toward the hearth. "Show me," he said. "Let me see what you brought me to trade for knowledge."

So, they did.

And something in the air beneath the trees, above the lazy river suggested that would be enough.

Jackson carried one of his finest handmade fishing poles—whittled from driftwood seasoned by sun and flood, the grain smooth from hours of carving. The line was braided twine, sturdy but flexible, and the lures—his Jackson Jones specials were forged from scrap wire and colored foil, tied with thread as fine as spider silk. The hooks, once razor sharp, had dulled with time and use, but they still gleamed with quiet threat. These weren't trinkets. They were survival.

Beth brought a cloth pouch, soft from years of use, filled with seed corn. Not for eating for planting. These kernels were gold for those who still believed the ground would yield. She understood the ritual: how to test for and tell the difference between growing soil and dirt, how to read seasons of when to plant and when to harvest. She knew the whispered steps of a harvest season like some kids knew pop songs.

And Bully brought flame. He carried a bow and spindle carved from river wood; the handles wrapped in scraps of hide. Moss and kindling were tucked carefully into the inner pocket of his coat, protected like something sacred. It was more than fire-starting gear. It was proof of self-reliance. A way to turn the cold earth into warmth with nothing but pressure and patience.

Beth greeted him with her name Beth Storm Chaser, and she untied her pouch and spilled the corn into her palm like she was holding jewels. She spoke softly about soil depth, germination, dry years and blight. She showed where the mold started, how to stop it before it spread. Knowledge passed like prayer.

Jackson stated he was Jackson Jones from Jonesboro; his mother was Māori from New Zealand and his father African American both died from a virus that claimed many adults and left children orphaned.

Jackson stepped forward and uncoiled his line, his rod steady in the dying light. He demonstrated the flick of the wrist, the curve of the hook. Then he pulled from his belt a battered pair of needle-nose pliers custom-made to dehook fish clean, efficiently. He held them out like a scalpel after he had caught that night's dinner for the four of them, right from the Missouri River.

Then Bully dropped to one knee beside the firepit. No words. Just the groan of wood against wood, the whisper of twine, the squeak of friction. Smoke rose slowly from the wood in the notch where he made a small nugget of fire and then he added tinder, curling into the gathering dark. And then flame as he blew on it. It caught like it always did. Bully was a true acolyte, a tender of the flame.

Laughter rose with it low and full. Not noisy. Not polite. Earned. Quinn reached behind a stack of buckets and pulled from his stash a bundle of dried meat, wrapped in wax cloth. He passed it around like it was a sacrament. No one spoke. They tore into it like communion, something more than sacred.

5

"Truth is the mirror that reflects our deepest selves."
unknown

Only when the last bite was swallowed did he finally extend his hand.

"Now," he said, grinning like the river itself had spoken, "show me what's got the ghosts of Spirit Mound stirring in their sleep."

Bully reached into the pouch and drew the coin out slowly, carefully as if it might change shape once revealed to air. He placed it into Quinn's waiting palm like an offering.

The hermit didn't speak right away.

He turned the coin over, fingers cradling it with a kind of quiet reverence. His brow furrowed, eyes narrowing beneath a sweep of dusk-colored lashes. In the firelight, the etching came alive: a coyote, poised on a rounded mound, tail arched, nose lifted toward the horizon of the moon. Latin script curved around the edge on the other side blank but for the delicate grooves of letters, like smoke caught in metal.

"Thesaurum Intra," Quinn murmured, voice caught halfway between memory and awe. "Treasure Within."

His thumb found the groove carved into the top of the coin a small notch, almost too perfect to be accidental. The metal pulsed faintly against his skin, or maybe it was just the heat of the fire reflected in his calloused fingers.

"You found this," Quinn said slowly, "on the trail to Spirit Mound?" Bully nodded. "Right near an obsidian rock I know that cause I traded the rock for food according to the owner of Muddy's. Shiny and Black as night with a streak of silver and large as my palm, quite heavy."

The hermit exhaled, long and slow through his nose, as if trying to empty something older than breath.

"Well then," he said, almost to himself, "let's stir up some ghosts." He tilted the coin to catch the firelight; the flicker carving shadows into the deep-cut lines. He turned it so all of them could see.

"The coyote," he said, "is more than a trickster, and this coyote might be a trickster, a Hayoka one who keeps evil away from that which is good. That's just what the frightened call him. What the wise know he's a guide. A survivor. A keeper of paths others forget."

He looked to Beth now, his eyes catching hers like a match held over dry bark.

"Vermillion, back before the curtain fell... the university mascot was the coyote. Funny how old signs echo forward, especially when no one's left to remember them, well I did."

His finger tapped the mound beneath the animal's feet.

"That's Spirit Mound. Or as the Lakota named it *Paha Wakan*. The sacred hill. Some say it hums when the moon is full. Some say it is a dream. But all the old stories agree it's protected."

Jackson leaned in. "Protected? By whom?"

Quinn's eyes didn't leave the coin. His voice dropped into something colder.

"Not who. What." He raised the coin, gold and shadow dancing across his face.

"The Little People. Eighteen inches tall. Fierce. Fast. Sharp as the flint they shoot. Not figments. Not metaphor. You don't walk into Paha Wakan without their permission. And you don't fool them. Some will see them as evil, but they are just protectors of the land."

He turned the coin once more in his fingers, the notch catching the light. Then, with a sudden weight that made the fire still, he looked back at Bully. "This notch at the top this is a key. To a lock created to be opened. It might open a door. A vision. A memory left buried in the bones of the land beneath Spirit Mound."

He handed the coin back, fingers lingering a second too long. "This place," he said softly, "isn't done talking. And it just spoke your name, Bully Everest."

He leaned forward then, resting his elbow on his knee, that crooked smile returning but the eyes, sharp as ever, scanned Bully's face for something deeper. Quinn's voice carried the weight of a challenge and the warmth of an old song. He wasn't demanding they could've left. But he expected, and somehow that meant more. Expectation was faith, wrapped in grit.

He rose slowly from his perch beside the fire, dusting ash from his palms. "You'll need more than guts," he added, voice low. "That coin's going to test who you are. Not just what you want."

Beth nodded, finishing her dinner. Jackson stared into the flames, already imagining the Little People reloading their arrows. And Bully he just tucked the coin back into its pouch, the weight of it like a heartbeat against his chest.

Quinn leaned back against the doorframe of his patchwork home, one eye squinting. "Spirit Mound's been waiting a long time," he said. "Just make sure when it asks its questions you answer honestly."

Then, with a sideways smile: "And when you come back if you come back, I want the whole story."

The night stretched around them. Stars blinked awake. And somewhere faint but real, the wind shifted—like something ancient had begun to listen.

6

"The path is not just a way forward; it's a way inward."

Unknown

The bike ride toward Spirit Mound began like so many other bike rides three friends just meandering across a wide, wind-bent prairie, neither hunted nor hurried, their silence companionable and a joke and laughter not serious. They moved loosely, untethered, their minds untwined from the moment. Above them, the clouds slid slowly and deliberate, stretching shadows across the grasslands like fingers brushing over memory.

None of them spoke too much.

Beth's thoughts spiraled around Quinn's words coyote, protector, treasure within trying to untangle truth from folklore.

Jackson kept scanning the horizon, tense, pretending not to be. At one point he cocked his head and muttered something about drums low, distant, tribal. He swore he heard them. Then dismissed it. Probably wind. Or nerves.

And Bully well Bully rode his bike with the quiet weight of the coin at his chest, the strap marking an X across his skin. He found himself wondering if all of this was just a long joke and one that history had played on them. Some forgotten ritual set into motion by someone two centuries gone and bored would be found laughing in their burial crypt.

The three of them got off their bikes at about the place where Bully found the Obsidian stone and pouch that hung around his neck. And together laughing as teens are want to do and they moved toward Spirit Mound carelessly.

The slope of Spirit Mound rose gently before them unimposing, ordinary, but buzzing with the subtle gravity of places that remember being sacred. The summit crept closer.

Then   Whirr.

A slicing sound, sharp and perfect, like a whisper turned blade.

Thunk.

Pain cracked open across Bully's forehead. Not deep, but sharp. Precise. The kind of sting that demanded attention.

He stumbled back, eyes wide, a sound like a hiss escaping his lips. His hands snapped to his brow. The arrow, a slip of wood no longer than a matchstick was lodged just above the bridge of his nose. Its obsidian tip still shimmered with intention.

Beth gasped, already stepping forward. Jackson froze, hand instinctively moving toward the knife strapped to his pack and the other hand to shield his eyes. All three moved away from the mound rather quickly.

Beth dropped low, her voice firm but calm. "Let's move back. Bully hold still. Just wait 'til you see this thing."

Bully dropped to one knee, his breath ragged, his vision swimming. Beth knelt in front of him, her fingers steady as stone, and cupped his head gently. One clean motion and the tiny dart came free.

Blood welled instantly as the forehead is a source of much bleeding in the right circumstances. A slender ribbon traced down his brow, over his nose and cheek, slipping past the corner of his mouth. It painted his face not with shame or injury, but with something ancient and ritual. The red lines curved like war paint, unplanned but perfect.

Beth didn't think. She dabbed the wound with the hem of her shirt and steadied Bully for a beat.

"You're alright," she whispered. "Just a scratch but yeah. They meant it."

That's when it began the chorus. Tiny voices rose from the rocks and tall grass. A million 18-inch warriors High-pitched. War-like. Delighted. Mocking laughter rang out all around them, unseen but undeniable.

The Little People, uh little devils, little warriors were watching. Jackson crouched now too, scanning the field. "Don't move," he muttered. "That wasn't a warning. That was a message."

Bully exhaled slowly through clenched teeth. The pain had sharpened something inside him. Focus like a blade. Beth placed a hand on his shoulder gentle, grounding.

"You're marked now, Everest. They see you. Stay here. Let us step ahead. Let's listen, for once." Bully nodded, wordless.

So Beth and Jackson moved toward the edge of the mound slow, measured, hearts pounding, but untouched. No arrow flew. No laughter followed. No little warriors.

The coin at Bully's chest vibrated softly, almost like breath. Not loud. Just present. He understood then it wasn't their footfalls that disturbed the guardians.

It was him. The key was already speaking. And the mountain, buried deep, had begun to answer. Bully didn't rush this time.

He moved through the grass like something older than a boy of fifteen measured, quiet, low to the ground. Each breath was deliberate. His eyes, half-lidded, swept the landscape without appearing to search. He sniffed the air not dramatic, not showy just enough to taste it. There was something in the wind. Wild. Ancient. He no longer treated it like a falsehood whispered between rusted doorframes. He knew this was real now.

The coin at his chest bounced gently with each step, tapping like a second heartbeat. His arms hung loose. His spine was steady. He wasn't charging toward battle he was joining it.

From twenty-five feet, he stopped low to the ground like a coyote might, smelled the air and circled back around.

A shadow skittered across a stone. A breeze curled around his hair, tugged once then passed. The air felt thick with waiting.

Twenty feet. The coin grew heavy or at least it was swaying more in the breeze. Or Bully was more aware of its weight. The drumming inside the mound grew louder no longer imagined. Rhythmic. Alive.

Fifteen feet. A sharp birdcall broke the air. And then heads. Tiny heads. Rising from the soil like prairie dogs, faces painted for war, eyes glinting obsidian. Silent. Watching.

Ten feet. Bully crouched. The air tightened. In unison, one million warriors unfolded across the hillside, every one of them drawing miniature arrows, ready for a second volley. Spears of tooth and flint. Too small to stop but too sharp to ignore.

Five feet. Bully crept closer, footfall feather-light. The warriors held their line, not moving, not blinking. They waited not for a sign of submission but something else.

Bully didn't need to turn to know Beth and Jackson were on the mound ahead of him. He could feel them like you feel the weight of a story at your back. The mound pulsed beneath his feet. This wasn't ground. It was memory, coiled and breathing.

A coyote wouldn't call out.

A coyote waits.

Until it doesn't. When the coyote senses the chicken, and with teasing motion finds its teeth around the neck. Bully feigning to be the coyote on the coin he did what no warrior would expect what only a trickster could.

He leaned forward, one foot over the mound's threshold, coin glinting from his chest in the leathered turtle. He lifted one leg as if to mark his territory, blood still trickling down his face like painted intent and loosed a sharp, wild howl. A cry that wasn't human, wasn't animal. Something in-between. Something old.

And the warriors a million or so erupted.

Not in fury. But in laughter. It made all three of the teens just laugh as well. Bully took the arrow to his forehead in stride.

High-pitched, rasping, gleeful, echoing laughter. The sound of rattlesnakes chuckling and owl bones clapping. The kind of laughter only heard when the trickster finally arrives at the celebration fashionably late, gloriously uninvited, and completely expected.

Bully Everest passed the first test.

7

"In the crucible of silence, the refiner waits not with wrath but with wonder." Unknown

One by one, the Little Warriors lowered their bows and sheathed their arrows.

A hundred thousand arrows were unstrung in perfect silence, each motion crisp, practiced, ancient. Then, without a word, the legion parted. They moved not like an army, but like a tide revealing a narrow path that led to a stone plate buried in the earth, worn smoothly by weather and memory.

At its center: a shallow indentation.

A notch.

Bully stepped forward. The coin in his hand hummed softly, the metal warming against his skin. He didn't hesitate. Didn't ask. He simply knelt and placed the coin into the slot. It clicked into place, like a heartbeat finding rhythm.

He turned it.

There was only one way it would go.

And when it turned the world shifted.

The ground trembled, low and deep, not like something breaking but something waking. The air grew cooler. The grass bent as if bowing. And then, with a grinding groan that split the silence like lightning across stone, the earth at the base of Spirit Mound pulled apart.

A chasm opened broad, clean, impossibly dark and from within it, a spiral staircase unfurled like a metal fern, ancient and waiting. Each step was carved into the earth itself, descending into depths that should not have existed beneath a Dakota hill much less Spirit Mound.

The three teens stood at the edge, the coin now back in Bully's pouch, still warm around his neck.

Around them, the Little Warriors began to vanish melting into the soil like shadows sliding into their source. Not retreating. Joining them.

Seeping into the descent.

8

**"Life is either a daring adventure or nothing at all."
Helen Keller**

And then the three stepped forward. First Beth, teeth clenched but eyes bright. Then Jackson, every step reluctant. And last, Bully laughing, not loud but true, like someone who had just unlocked the dream that had followed him since birth.

When the last foot touched the stairs, the earth above groaned again.

And sealed.

Gone was the sky. The prairie. The mound.

Just darkness now. And the descent.

Jackson's voice echoed small in the vast hollow. "Uh. I'm afraid of the dark."

Beth pressed closer, trying not to brush the walls. "And I don't like creepy crawly things."

Bully said nothing.

Just kept walking, the coin now glowing faintly in his pouch, laughter curling in his chest like a firelight behind a closed door.

And down they went into the marrow of the legend, where no path could be retraced.

33

They were still catching their breath when the earth betrayed them.

Without warning, the solid stairs beneath their feet buckled, softened melted. Stone became slick as glass, and the three teens pitched forward with startled yelps, careening down a spiraling chute carved smoothly by time and design. It wasn't chaos. It was orchestration deliberate descent on a slide into the heart of Spirit Mound.

They landed roughly on top of each other but alive on a narrow ledge of stone jutting out into a vast subterranean chamber. The ceiling disappeared into shadow; the floor, if there was one, was lost beneath mist and black. The ledge was barely wide enough for three bodies to balance. Behind them? A drop that sang of forever.

In front of them, suspended across a great angled floor of stone that sloped upward at a cruel incline, glowed a small red coal embedded in a distant wall. It shimmered like a heartbeat unreachable. At their feet, nestled in a rock niche, lay a quiver of ten arrows and a bow. Nothing else.

Ten arrows.

Three of them.

Beth saw it first. Her breath caught. "A trial uh a test," she said quietly. "That's what this is."

They understood: the target must be struck. The cost of failure meant distance as each miss carried you further from the mark. It would take focus. Luck. Precision.

Beth stepped forward. Her fingers knew the bow, remembered its curve. She took the first arrow, notched it with care, and fired.

Wide right. Clean miss.

The floor under her tilted suddenly—like a breath exhaled from stone. With a yelp, she slipped and slid backwards, disappearing into the slope and falling exactly fifty yards further down the incline before catching herself, breathless.

Jackson stepped forward next, teeth clenched. His shot missed too left and short. Down he went.

Bully tried. His arrow hit nothing, nowhere. And like the others, he was swept fifty yards away.

Then, impossibly, the bow and quiver reappeared in front of them—untouched. Whole. Without three arrows.

Beth climbed back to shoot again. This time, her arrow arched high and true—nearly perfect—but missed just above the burning coal. She cursed softly, fists tight. Another slide. Another descent.

Jackson studied her angle, tried to replicate it—but his arrow slipped from his fingers mid-release, and he was given one more. It skittered uselessly across the floor. Down he went.

Bully exhaled. A long, slow breath. His second attempt missed so wildly that from the dark above them, the Little People burst into laughter—tiny, wicked joy echoing from the shadows. He grinned. Even failure could be funny.

The trial was unkind. Each miss sent them deep fifty yards, then another fifty, and another. Until only three arrows remained. And only one figure stood at the top.

Beth's third shot trembled with fatigue. Her arms wobbled. The arrow veered sideways almost hitting Jackson mid-stumble. Her scream of frustration was muffled by her next fall.

Jackson shook, palms sweating. His grip slipped again. The arrow flew wrong, skidding to rest with a pathetic tap.

Gone. Both. Swallowed by the slope. Lost in the distance.

Only Bully remained. Bully couldn't hear his friends.

He stepped forward.

One arrow left. One heartbeat. The fire in the wall stared back at him, unblinking.

He took a breath that went deeper than his lungs dared breathe in. His hands were steady now. Not because he was unafraid but because he understood. The coin at his chest throbbed softly, matching the pulse of the target ahead.

He pulled the string.

And let go.

Silence.

Then impact.

A crack of red light, pure and clean. The arrow sank deep into the center of the coal, extinguishing it in a blink of gold flame. From the shadows, the warriors erupted not with mocking laughter but exultation. Cheers, whoops, wild tiny drumbeats bouncing across the cavern ceiling.

And in an instant, the slope beneath them smoothed and flattened. Beth, Jackson, and Bully stood side by side again, now on a platform lit with shifting luminous colors amber, green, blue, violet. Like stained glass woven from light.

10

"Until you step into the unknown, you don't know what you're made of." Roy T. Bennett

In the center of the stone floor stood a pedestal. Upon it: a hollow shaped perfectly for a coin.

Bully stepped forward, fingers wrapped around the pouch, and he released the coin into his hand, the groove still warm from the last lock it had turned. He held it steadily, then pressed it into the second keyhole nestled in the stone pedestal. It fit with a whisper, then clicked with the certainty of design older than anyone alive could explain.

He turned it.

It only moved one way.

The sound followed not loud, but immense. Like stone remembering how to breathe. Deep within the cavern, gears of rock groaned to life, ancient mechanisms awakened from long sleep. The echo rolled toward them, low and rumbling, like thunder in the bones of the earth.

Then came the grind of something moving.

From the far end of the chamber, a massive sphere hewn from solid stone, perfectly smooth began to roll forward along a hidden track. The noise built steadily as it approached, louder with each heartbeat, until it came to an abrupt, dead halt directly in front of them.

Still.

Waiting.

Without hesitation, Bully stepped up, the coin cradled in his palm. He reached out, touched the curved face of the stone sphere, and pressed the coin into a shallow slot that had not existed a breath earlier. A seam split down the center with a soft hiss and compressed air hissed out.

The stone unfolded like petals under invisible instruction, revealing what lay at the heart of it. Inside: a helmet.

Not just any helmet but a pilot's helmet, clearly built for a suit, its surface was time-worn, the visor tinted gold like fire trapped in amber. Its shape was utilitarian, but its soul was something else entirely.

On the side, painted with precision and pride, was the stylized image of an eagle majestic and upright, dressed in the regalia of ceremony. Feathers cascading in careful rows. Eyes sharp with clarity. It bore the hallmarks of

Lakota, Nakota, and Dakota artistry symbols passed down through generations. This wasn't just a bird.

It was heritage, enshrined in machinery.

And just beneath the crest, faded but unmistakable: the classic NASA worm script. Curving white letters that once dreamed of stars now whispered of purpose here underground.

A name was stenciled along the crown in small, steady font:

Chief Red Herringbone, M.D. Pilot. Architect. Witness.

Mars explorer.

The helmet pulsed faintly in the dark as if it had simply been waiting for hands worthy, for myth to reach back, for the right voice to wear it again.

Waiting.

As Bully wrapped his fingers around the helmet, the vault lights surged not in blinding brilliance, but in something melodic. Radiant, golden, like the final chord of a song that had waited centuries for its ending note. The chamber didn't tremble. It exhaled.

Beneath their feet, the stone platform stirred.

Not a quake. A lift.

The earth peeled upward, graceful and deliberate, stone unfurling like a blooming petal. Light streamed from invisible seams as the trio rose not with jolt or noise, but with the ease of something carried by the breath of the mountain itself.

And then from the cracks and corners of the sacred vault they emerged.

The Little Warriors.

A million of them, scrambling from stone like sparks, faces marked in fierce patterns of coal and clay. They wore breastplates crafted from chiton shells, feathers sewn into bands on their tiny brows. Arrows no longer than needles gleamed at their backs, tips glinting like obsidian teeth kissed by sunlight.

They poured from crevices in joyous chaos climbing one another's shoulders, waving miniature flags stitched from scavenged cloth and bone-thread. Their drums, beaten beetle-shells strung with spider silk, boomed with wild rhythm. They tumbled, danced, and flipped midair. They sang in a tongue older than bark, older than rivers, a language that didn't care if it was understood only that it was heard.

By the time the platform breached the surface, Spirit Mound was no longer still.

It danced.

Not in fire, but in motion. In ceremony. The Little People moved like a tide, sweeping outward, their bodies a blur of rhythm and light. They formed a circle that spiraled, pulsed, laughed itself into the dusk wider than wind, older than time.

Beth stood wide-eyed, frozen between awe and disbelief. Jackson looked like he might faint or dance, depending on what the music told him next.

And Bully, helmet in hand, mouth still split in disbelief, could only shake his head and shout over the rhythm, "Okay. I've seen a lot of weird things. But this—this is certified next level weird."

And the Little Warriors roared in agreement.

When Bully placed the helmet over his head, it didn't resist. The fit adjusted seamlessly, like it had waited generations for the shape of Bully's skull. The inner lining flexed and sealed, molding to bone and memory.

A soft click. Then crackle. With that click a small needle like insertion that was barely felt but enough of a jolt to awaken Bully to ask the question "What?"

Sound burst through the speakers tucked behind his ears dusty, brittle, like an old radio tuning across years. The visor flared to life in a wash of golden blue, and the world outside melted into light.

Inside the glass, a desert unfolded. At first, nothing but wind and dusk. Then movement. A figure on four legs: a coyote, walking slowly toward a fireless circle of stones. As it drew closer, it shimmered, its body stretching, unfurling.

41

The coyote stood and became a man.

A tall, aging man, draped in ceremonial cloth and worn leather, feathers braided into his greying hair. His eyes were weathered but bright. His posture, precise. He smiled and bowed ever so slightly.

"Hau, Tanyan Yahi," he said a greeting in Lakota, warm and formal. "I welcome you, who have come far."

The voice was rich, grounded, more felt than heard.

"My name is Chief Red Herringbone, M.D. My message comes from the year 2080 a dispatch across time, for those brave or wild enough to carry the coin. Tell me, my friend what is your name?"

Bully hesitated, then answered, his voice calmed inside the hum of the helmet.

"My two friends named me Bully Everest. I found the coin buried beneath the black obsidian rock on the trail to Spirit Mound and I guess you must have placed that rock and coin a long time ago."

Chief Red Herringbone nodded slowly, smiling wider. "Of course, I did bury it and of course it was you who found it. Spirit Mound still calls to the right souls. And you've passed the tests that we left in place."

His tone shifted slightly lower, edged with concern.

"But be warned. If the Government of Gold still breathes even in whispers, then you are not free of danger. The real trial begins now. The game of shadows is patient."

There was a pause. Chief Red said, "What year is this?"

Bully swallowed. "Twenty-two fifty uh 2 2 5 0."

A long exhale from Herringbone. Not surprisingly but filled with sadness.

"Then the Government of Gold lived longer than we feared."

"Yes," Bully said. "We don't hear much from the Government of Gold these days. Beth, Jackson, and I are just orphans in what's left of South Dakota. Desert waste. Dust and sky. We live in a greenhouse somewhere between what used to be Yankton and Vermillion, near the Missouri River."

Red Herringbone's expression shifted, something like pride slipping beneath grief. "Then you are exactly who we hoped for."

Chief Red Herringbone's voice crackled gently in Bully's ear, calm but laced with a sense of quiet urgency.

"I'll need to catalogue not just you," he said, "but your two companions as well. If you're willing, allow this helmet to be placed on each of your friends' heads."

Bully gave a slow nod—and without further motion, he removed the helmet and gave it to Beth and the Helmet like it had done on Bully clicked into place and a small crackle, and the insertion of a small needle where Beth also yelped, "what?" and then introductions and the process and same response happened with Jackson as well .

With the helmet on their heads, Beth Storm Chaser and Jackson Jones appeared in the helmet's display—framed in soft light, eyes wide with wonder, their names etched in elegant script like honorary titles in a registry of legend. Beth, with her braid tangled and wild; Jackson, leaning just slightly forward as if ready to run or dream. Red's voice greeted each in turn, warm and clear.

"Well met, Beth Storm Chaser. Jackson Jones. You've been seen." Jackson took the helmet off and they could still see and hear Chief Red Herringbone MD as if he were right in front of them. He was in their peripheral vision.

11

"Faith means living with uncertainty feeling your way though life, letting your heart guide you like a lantern in the dark." Dan Millman

Then Chief Red Herringbone MD straightened at least, the version of him inside the projection did and gestured toward a distant horizon beyond the digital dusk.

"There are two more yet to find," he said, "and I believe you three are meant to help them. But first you'll need to travel west."

His image shifted, and the helmet's lens bloomed into a topographic map its contours alive with motion. Mountains swelled like clenched fists. Plains rippled like breath on glass. He tapped a pulsing point, faintly glowing like a heartbeat.

"Belle Fourche, South Dakota. Beneath the Center of the Nation monument," he said. "My friends and I carved a slide not for amusement, though I won't lie, it's a hell of a ride. Gravity-forged. Magnet-guided. Cushioned by engineered gel. If you're game, it'll take you there in a few hours and your first trip you will find rest like you never have before, but before I take you, all of you need to say is you are willing to be on this journey, and it is risky and you could die." So just place your finger on top of the helmet where my name is and your name will be added to the journey

Bully glanced at the others. "What do you think?"

Beth's grin arrived before the words. Jackson just bared his teeth in a wolfish smile. "We've already fallen through one prairie dog hole," he said. "What's one more?"

Each placed their thumb on the name of Chief Red Herringbone, MD and their names were added to the helmet.

Then came the sound.

12

"Exploring the unknown requires tolerating uncertainty." Brian Greene

High and thin at first, like a mosquito whine. Then sharper. Heavier. Drones sleek, silent predators split the sky overhead, their silver forms darting like hawks in formation.

"They've found Spirit Mound," Red said, voice tightening by a thread. "You'll want to move. Now."

The earth trembled not in panic, but in permission. Spirit Mound folded inward, petals sealing shut, and the three teens dropped into its core drawn down, deeper, faster, as if gravity had remembered them.

At the bottom: a vessel that defied simple category. Sleek as a shadow, resting on a magnetic rail that hummed with anticipation. Not quite a car. Not a train. Something older but to them something new and amazing. Something waiting.

The hatch opened.

Inside: three seats, sculpted like open palms. Light pulsed and lit the floor, alive with directional flow. The walls pulsed with velocity, promising something between speed and surrender.

They climbed in.

As drones swept above, casting eyes through branches and heat signatures, the trio vanished into the earth slingshot into the bones of the continent, racing west, toward a destination that once marked unity and now whispered ruin.

Toward Belle Fourche.
Toward the center of a nation no longer united or whole or on the map, of something long buried but not gone.
Toward whatever waited.

Above, silence fractured.

Far from Spirit Mound and its hidden rail, the Government of Gold stirred. Not with an alarm. But with precision.

Within the darkened command chamber—a vault beneath a forgotten dam—rows of dim-eyed analysts traced new movement. One blip. Then two. Then three. Power readings not seen in generations. Uncatalogued. Untouchable.

A flicker of the old world. The Protocol hadn't called it by name in years, but the algorithm knew the shape of insurgency. This wasn't noise. This was memory waking up.

No nuclear strike—too costly. Too conspicuous. South Dakota didn't hold enough living bodies to warrant the expense. But the directive came quickly:

Unrestricted resource clearance.
Global satellite refocused
Scan for myth, keyword, forgotten names.

No signal would hide. No story would go untracked.

And somewhere deep inside the drone matrix, a file unlocked red coded, high priority.

Target Designation: Three unidentified. Two male, one female. Dead or Alive. Authorized Agent: Wade Castle, Sergeant of Arms.

Castle had been waiting for a hunt. Former soldier. Current ghost. His ethics were archived centuries ago. He didn't ask questions. He simply pointed, clicked, and erased.

Within the hour, he was airborne inside a retrofitted war drone, slicing northwest from the Florida wastes.

The chase had resumed.
And the gold no longer gleamed. The Government of Gold burned to end the possibility of hope.

End of Chapter Book 1

"The world is round and the place which may seem like the end may also be only the beginning." Rebecca West

Thesaurum Intra Book 2

Prologue

"Every new beginning comes from some other beginnings end." Seneca the Younger

Since you have been reading and then you heard about the Government of Gold and my own AI consciousness is similar to the current AI consciousness of the President who is still president in the year 2250 two hundred years after he created the perfect coup.

You might think I am talking about another golden president but that is not it at all.

President Gold and I, being Chief Red Herringbone MD were civil servants, he was the bureaucratic end of the space program to Mars and I was one of three space engineers used with NASA, JAXA, and Roscosmos.

My two friends were Japanese and Ukrainian, and they both defected not by choice but because they couldn't leave the United States following our final trip home from the Mars Space Station.

At first glance, you might assume I have been talking about the government of Gold as being about President Donald J. Trump 45th and 47th President of the United States but President Gold was the 50th President of the United States of America and last President, and indeed, the comparison to Malcom Buster Gold is tempting.

Both were populists who thrived on spectacle, disruption, and a defiant connection to their base.

But while President Trump may have catalyzed the societal unraveling that set the stage for Gold's ascent, it was Malcom Buster Gold Texas-born, independently elected, and a millionaire larger than life who truly shattered the foundations.

His middle name, Buster, became both his brand and his warning. Critics mocked him as all bluster, but underneath the bravado was a mind far more dangerous than Trump's. Where Trump dabbled in manipulation with surface-level cunning, Gold played the long game.

After serving a single term, Malcom Buster Gold didn't step away from power he eclipsed the republic. With chilling precision, he brought the United States to its knees not with military might, but by severing its digital arteries.

In the space of weeks, the infrastructure that once hummed beneath every phone call, power line, and screen went dark. President Trump had thrived within the glow of constant connection, but Gold understood that true dominance wasn't built on visibility. It thrived in silence.

At the heart of the blackout sat Gold himself, hands steady on the levers of collapse. While the public panicked and scrambled for answers, he operated in the static, orchestrating a series of invisible assassinations.

There were no headlines, no public reckonings, only absence. Entire lines of opposition vanished, their erasure known only to the few who dared keep count.

But here's where it twisted further: the unplugging wasn't total. It was targeted. Gold had preserved a walled-off grid for his inner circle an insulated sanctum of high-functioning tech and surveillance, untouched by the falling of the curtain. This was the scaffolding of a new regime, one built not on democratic pretense, but on precision fear.

AI systems once public servants were retooled as predators. Drones traced invisible grids in the sky. Cameras rooted themselves into every blind corner. Gold's government didn't announce itself; it watched.

Society, stripped of convenience, cracked under the silence. The common person no longer drove fuel, and function belonged to the state. If you couldn't repair a bike or tame a horse, you didn't move. Civilization shrank to footpaths and whispers, while above, the eyes of the new order never blinked.

Even in death, President Malcom Buster Gold refused to relinquish power. Before his body expired, he ensured his mind would not. Through a process known only to a cloistered sect of post-human engineers, a digital simulacrum of Gold was encoded—his decision-making, his rhetoric, even his unpredictability preserved in a self-learning intelligence known simply as The Protocol.

It didn't govern through charisma anymore, it governed through memory, menace, and unyielding logic. Two centuries had passed since the coup, but the world still trembled beneath the boot print of a man long buried. His directives encoded at the end of his flesh-bound life became the scaffolding for a regime that spanned not just borders, but generations. Gold, no longer a man, had become the firmware of civilization.

In the chaotic decades that followed his death, small flames of resistance flickered settlements in the hills of former Appalachia, communes in the deserts beyond Nevada's reach, hidden conclaves along the old river systems. These were the dreamers, the descendants of those who remembered freedom. But dreams had no place under the eyes of The Protocol.

Orbiting satellites identified patterns. There was a surge in radio frequency here, an unexpected clustering of biometric signals there. The AI didn't see people. It saw anomalies. And one by one, those anomalies were corrected. Not with strikes, but with silence. Entire counties of people were swallowed by unmarked nuclear detonations, no warning, no broadcast. Just heat and erasure. To preserve order, the system removed disorder. Permanently.

The world forgot rebellion not through indoctrination, but through absence. Children were born who had never heard of dissent. Cities thrived under glass skies, sterile and obedient. And yet somewhere, beneath it all, an echo remained.

1

**"In the midst of Chaos, there is also opportunity."
Sun Tzu**

Sergeant-at-Arms Wade Castle was a New Marine by classification, but to most, he was a shadow carved from war itself. Standing just over six feet tall, his frame was sculpted from a fusion of reinforced tissue and exo-armor a seamless blend of body and machine. He didn't just wear his armor. He *was* the armor.

Built for pursuit, bred for precision, Castle didn't hunt targets; he dismantled them. Killing wasn't a mission it was a language he spoke fluently, and he took grim pleasure in each syllable.

He always wore mirrored glasses, as much for psychological warfare as concealment. No one had truly seen his eyes in decades. But when his systems fully activated, when the mission pulled him into peak operational intensity, those lenses glowed from beneath— deep red. Like warning beacons. Like anger given form.

Rumor said he didn't sleep, didn't eat, didn't speak unless the moment demanded it. But everyone knew this: if Wade Castle was sent after you, you weren't just a fugitive. You were already dead.

2

"All warfare is based on deception." Sun Tzu

Bully Everest didn't dare question Chief Red not out loud at least not yet. So, with a mix of confusion and awe, he clambered into the impossibly sleek vehicle that looked more like a dream than a machine.

It wasn't just a vehicle; it was a gravity-scoffing miracle, designed to pierce the crust of the Earth and plunge them deep toward some inverted gravitational point under South Dakota to the center of where?

For a kid who'd never piloted more than a rusty bike over dirt roads, this was a plunge into the sublime. The moment he sat, the seat responded with tendrils of intelligent mesh unfurling like living vines, wrapping around him, cradling him.

He gasped as it formed a second skin, cocooning him in comfort and control, holding him fast so he wouldn't so much as jostle when the journey began. Beth and Jackson squirmed at first too, but the seats knew their bodies, adjusting with eerie precision.

Chief Red hadn't just designed transportation he'd built connection. Without so much as a helmet click, they were linked, neural threads whispering silently between their minds. A micro-injection, no sharper than a mosquito's kiss, had embedded circuitry into their skulls the moment they entered. And now, even a glance from one fed into the others' visual field.

The car wasted no time. As it sped downward through impossible strata, the mesh began unraveling their old clothes not tearing them, but absorbing them, breaking them down. In their place grew suits of engineered fiber, responsive to touch, crafted from the castoff debris of their own bodies: dead skin, sweat, carbon. It was resourceful and brilliant.

The suits formed like second skin, customized mid-journey colors chosen by each of them in whichever environment they were in and when offered a choice, shoes all part of one garment adjusted to mood, visors tailored to their emerging roles.

It felt less like dressing and more like becoming. For Bully Everest, who'd never dreamt of entering a world beyond his prairie existence, this wasn't just a ride. It was a rebirth.

As the vehicle tilted into its downward arc, something subtle and deeply natural but forgotten began to unfold. A cool mist kissed their ankles at first, barely more than vapor. But soon, a slow tide of pale blue liquid oxygen crept up around their feet, rising like a tide inside the compartment.

The teens might have panicked; anyone who were in the shoes of these teens would have panicked, but the vehicle had anticipated that. A lullaby of bio-feedback pulses calmed their minds, slowly folding their consciousness into sleep. It was the only way to protect them. Awake, their hearts would have rebelled under the stress of transformation, and they would have died.

Because this was no ordinary oxygen. It had been infused engineered at the molecular level with a symbiotic genetic key. As the liquid climbed past their knees, then chest, then faces, it began to bond with their altered DNA, seeping through skin like breath through lung. They weren't drowning, they were adapting.

Their bodies became sponges for the element, cellular walls softening, allowing exchange at a microscopic level. And in this perfect suspension pressurized, nutrient-rich, precisely calibrated they began to shed illness like old skin. Every fever, every allergy, every lingering weakness they were purged, rewritten. Not just healed. Upgraded.

The gel was more than transport it was transformation.

As the vessel propelled itself through one ancient subterranean tunnel, its interior became almost organic. The walls pulsed with a bioluminescent glow, the floor yielding softly beneath them like muscle under skin. Suspended inside was a translucent gel cool, dense, and gently undulating like a living tide.

The teens, still asleep, drifted within it not floating, not drowning, but absorbing. The gel wasn't inert; it was engineered, infused with a molecular thread drawn from one of the planet's most resilient lifeforms: the tardigrade. Within the fluid matrix, strands of dormant DNA began knitting into their cells, silent upgrades woven into their biology.

It wasn't about strength or speed. This was a deeper resilience. Cellular reprogramming that would let them endure extremes no human had ever faced with pressure, radiation, temperature, even time. Their organs slowed. Their immune systems rebooted. And somewhere deep within their rewritten code, a dormant spark awaited its first trial.

The membrane that formed the interior of the ride flexed around them adaptable, pliant, intelligent. It allowed the three to remain in proximity without disruption, adjusting for movement, weight, breath. Encased in the gel, they were both isolated and connected, dreaming beneath the earth in a shared cocoon of evolution.

By the time they reached their destination, the metamorphosis would be complete.

They didn't know it yet, but when they awoke, they would be something new. More than human. Not quite alien. But perfectly attuned to the world below and above.

The shift from liquid to air hit them like a whispered alarm subtle at first, then undeniable. As the gel receded from their lungs and was replaced with oxygen, each of them jolted awake in a shared, silent panic. Reflexes flared, hearts surged, but their bodies reengineered and calmed by the transition held firm. They didn't drown. They reemerged.

The capsule's interior softened its glow as the pressure equalized. Lights danced briefly over surfaces like the fading pulse of the vessel itself, and the gel that had cradled them for hours now drained away, leaving their skin tingling, their muscles humming with new density.

They survived the dive. But more than that they'd changed.

Before any of them could speak, a familiar voice filled the chamber. Chief Red Herringbone, MD, medical architect of their journey, hadn't waited for full lucidity.

"Don't panic. That breath you just took. It's your first as something more refined," Chief Red said, his voice threading through the neural link rather than the air. "The liquid oxygen wasn't just for survival it was a carrier. You've been modified at the cellular level. Your new physiology mimics some of the most resilient organisms on Earth. Tardigrade-inspired adaptations: pressure tolerance, metabolic stasis, radiation resistance, even enhanced regenerative capacity. And yes baby-soft skin," he added with a dry chuckle.

Bully blinked. Beth flexed her fingers. Jackson's gaze darted instinctively toward the helmet, but it remained untouched, resting beside them. And yet, their connection was intact.

Red continued. "The neural insertion barely the width of a human hair remains your conduit. It allows sensory relay, cognitive tuning, and shared awareness. You're not just altered. You're bonded. The world you're about to enter doesn't bend to the weak, but you won't need to survive it. You were built to thrive in it."

The capsule gave a soft shudder. A hatch unsealed with a slow hiss. They'd slept through the descent. Now they would step into something far stranger than sleep could ever prepare them for.

Chief Red Herringbone, MD, had a habit, some would say a compulsion for quoting the greats. It was how he anchored purpose into motion, how he turned confusion into momentum. And today, with three teens barely out of suspended animation and barely into their training, was no different.

He stood before them, hands behind his back, voice steady. "As General Colin Powell once said, 'A dream doesn't become reality through magic; it takes sweat, determination, and hard work.' From this point forward, that's your currency sweat, determination, and hard work. You've been altered but not completed. I'm here to shape you into what you were always meant to be: a team."

Jackson groaned, rubbing the side of his head. "I'm still trying to remember how to blink. Maybe let us breathe normal air for a second before the motivational montage?"

Beth chuckled, still stretching the last of the stasis out of her spine. "Yeah, Coach. Maybe after we've had a meal that isn't molecular gel?"

Even Bully, ever stoic, allowed a dry smile. "Not everyone adjusts to genetic upgrades before breakfast."

Chief Red didn't miss a beat. He walked a slow arc in front of them, the hint of a smirk under his silvered beard. "'Believe you can and you're halfway there.' President Roosevelt said that. And I expect you to meet me at halfway awake or not."

A silence hung for half a second—then Jackson shrugged. "Fine. But if we're finding this fourth team member of yours, they better have snacks."

3

"let your plans be dark and impenetrable as night, and when you move, fall like a thunderbolt." Sun Tzu

It had been twenty-four hours since the teens vanished beneath the Earth's skin, swallowed by an ancient arc of gravity no one alive could trace. Above ground, under a flat gray sky that carried the weight of a coming storm, Sergeant-at-Arms Wade Castle stood still at the edge of Spirit Mound.

He was not frustrated. Wade Castle didn't indulge in frustration. But something in the silence gnawed at him. No scorch marks. No footprints. No energy signatures left behind. Just wind, dust, and a sacred hill that had sealed itself like a wound and three left behind rusting bicycles.

He didn't rely on instinct alone he was built for precision. Castle deployed a fleet of sentient drones, each tuned to different spectrums: thermal, chemical, and psionic. They didn't just scan they inquired. Pieced together local chatter, overheard murmurs, read the tremble in a heartbeat.

"Build the profile," he ordered.

They would find everything names, habits, dietary records, family branches, digital ghosts. The algorithm didn't stop at what people said, it unraveled what they remembered and what they forgot to hide.

But that was only one front.

While the machines buzzed overhead and the first heavy excavators rumbled toward Spirit Mound an act of desecration he didn't blink at Castle walked. On foot, tracing a faint line where bicycle tires had once etched the earth. Old-fashioned tracking. Tire treads through silt. Crushed grass. The logic of movement.

He spoke to no one at first, then began interviewing the fringe dwellers, those who made homes near the edge of forgotten places. He didn't threaten. He didn't need to. His presence alone was pressure.

Something had moved beneath this land.

And Castle intended to follow it into the dark.

4

"Appear weak when you are strong, and strong when you are weak." Sun Tzu

Skinny Colley all white hair, long white beard crouched low beside a sputtering fire pit near the dry edge of the Belle Fourche River a name it barely earned now, the water little more than a stubborn trickle through cracked earth. The meat on the skewers sizzled, thin strips of squirrel turning crisp over the flame, their scent hovering somewhere between desperation and determination.

He squinted into the smoke, voice gravelly. "Yo! Bring me the seasoning. If I'm gonna chew this leathery runt, it better not taste like the rest of the trash we've been scraping up."

From the doorway of their leaning shack, his daughter called back lazily, "Pops, just relax. Let the fire work its magic. Heat tames everything if you're patient."

Yoshiko appeared a moment later, her stride unhurried and assured. She wore old blue jeans that had gone soft from too many washes, a pair of cowboy boots that had long since lost their shine, and a pearl-snap shirt faded from sun and soot. Her battered Stetson was tilted back on her head, revealing a tangle of jet-black hair braided down her spine, the braid brushing her waist like a trail of quiet fire.

She handed over the seasoning with a smirk. "You act like squirrel's supposed to taste like steak."

Skinny took it without looking, muttering under his breath. "I just want it to taste like not defeat for once."

The fire cracked. Somewhere in the distance, a drone hummed low and uncertain like it wasn't sure it belonged out here.

The platform ascended in silence, a phantom elevator returning from the bones of the world. As it rose through the tunnel's narrow throat, the air thinned and cooled, and the glow of the cavern below gave way to starlight bleeding through cracks above.

The three teens stood still, no longer wrapped in rags or scavenged layers. Now they wore smooth, skin-tight unitards colorless, seamless, designed to vanish into the dark. They looked like shadows given shape, half-human, half-myth, standing in formation as the platform breached the surface.

It emerged onto a long-abandoned street, Aurora Street off the beaten path in Belle Fourche. In the early days of the Government of Gold, this street carried no generations.

Families didn't gather here, markets didn't bloom, laughter always once echoed between brick walls. That was in 2080, when people still pretended life could be normal. Before the whispers stopped. Before the cities forgot their own names.

Now, the ruins stood quiet, layered in dust and time.

To the north, barely visible in the moonlight, a narrow tributary curled through the earth like a memory—the beautiful fork where the red water river and Belle Fourche rivers intertwined for which the city had once been named. It shimmered faintly, reflecting stars no one had looked up to in years.

The platform locked into place with a soft mechanical sigh. The teens stepped off into the cool night air, lungs filled with breath from another era.

They were above ground again. And nothing would be the same.

Nothing about this place felt familiar. The stars wheeled in the sky above them as if the constellations had shifted while they slept. They didn't know how far they'd travelled, only that they weren't where they began. If this truly was Belle Fourche, it bore no sign of the world it used to be. Just ruins, silence, and the faint smell of something meaty cooking over fire.

GoG short for the Government of Gold was never far from their thoughts. It would follow, relentless and quiet. But what they didn't know, couldn't know, was that there was someone far worse than drones or protocols tracking them now. An assassin didn't wait for orders. He pursued them like an echo trailing a heartbeat.

Bully tightened the straps on the backpack, the one with the helmet and took in the scent curling through the dusk. Hunger gnawed deeper than curiosity. They were about to step forward when a voice, rough and steady as gravel under boot, called out from the shadows.

"Hands up. Drop the bag. Step into the firelight nice and slow."

The three froze like deer caught in a field.

A figure emerged lean, sure, dust covered. She wore worn jeans and scuffed boots that had survived generations. A weathered shotgun rested steady in her arms, its metal dulled by time but impeccably clean. The hat on her head cast a long shadow across her face, but the braid down her spine gleamed beneath the moonlight.

"I said now, strangers."

They obeyed partly out of caution, partly instinct. And partly because, though Yoshiko couldn't see or hear him, Chief Red's voice echoed through their neural thread with crisp authority.

"She's not bluffing. Do as she says. No sudden moves."

So, they did. Bully dropped the pack. Beth raised her hands with a twitch of nerves. Jackson exhaled slowly, eyes trained on the flickering firelight ahead saw the skewered meat cooking over the fire and a whitehaired and wild white beard of a man laughing at them all.

The fire crackled. The shotgun didn't waver.

And somewhere behind Yo's unshaken gaze, a question was already forming: Who were these three, and why did they look like transformation?

Yoshiko eyed the trio with a narrowed gaze that didn't quite reach suspicion curiosity kept it in check. Their clothing was like nothing she'd seen: seamless, fluid, almost too perfect. Not flashy, but efficient like armor disguised as cloth. Their faces were eerily smooth, unmarred by sun or scar, as if history had not yet touched them.

Too clean, she thought. Too untouched for this dust bitten world.

Red Herringbone's voice stirred in the teens' neural threads, quiet and observational. She's sharp. Reads deeper than most. And she's not who she pretends to be.

She moved with the confidence of someone raised among cattle and firelight, boots worn but sure, hat cocked back to reveal a braid like a black ribbon trailing down her back. But Red sensed more a genealogy that didn't quite match the white-haired man she called "Pops." Her features echoed East Asia: high cheekbones, almond eyes sharp with calculation. Japanese, perhaps. Maybe Korean. And yet she was all cowboy an archivist of the old codes, keeper of a defunct library system that, ironically, held more human knowledge than any remaining node in the Government of Gold's data net.

She leveled her shotgun just slightly higher. "Who are you and why here, now?"

Bully raised his hands slowly. "If we told you, I'm not sure you'd believe us."

Jackson added, "Also, if you're not going to shoot us, could we maybe please have a bite of whatever you've got cooking? We haven't had anything that smells like food in two days."

Beth, ever the disarming one, flashed a grin. "Love the hat, by the way."

Yoshiko didn't lower the weapon. But her mouth twitched just a little.

"Cute," she said. "You look like ghosts, talk like time travelers, and compliment my fashion sense while trespassing on my firelight."

She paused, studying them one by one. Then, to no one in particular: "Pops always said the weird ones are the ones worth listening to. Alright. Come closer, but slowly. And no sudden moves."

She stepped back, just enough for the firelight to catch the edges of their new suits shimmering faintly under ash and starlight.

Something told her this story was going to be very, very old and entirely new.

"Put the gun down, Yo," Skinny said, voice calm but firm. "They're not here to hurt us. And just look at 'em—they're dressed like something outta of a dream... or a fever vision."

Yoshiko's shotgun lowered slowly, reluctantly as Skinny stepped forward and gave the strangers a nod. "Truth is, you three might be safer with us than out there. This stretch of land's crawling with all kinds of trouble these days. Crazy cowboys, tech-wild scavengers... and worse."

He gestured toward the fire. "Come on then. Pull up a seat. There's more than enough."

The skewers hissed, spitting the scent of squirrel fat into the night air. "Bagged about thirty of these little beasts this week," he said proudly. "Smoked and salted 'em down some for us, some to trade. Not glamorous, but it'll keep you standing."

He gave them a warm smile and nodded toward the girl beside him. "Name's Skinny. This is my daughter, Yoshiko Sensei. Found her abandoned when she was just a babe. Took her in best I could. Didn't have much then. Don't have much now. But I taught her to ride, to ranch, to shoot straighter than most men twice her size. And more importantly she's the only one around here who can read a book without squinting." He laughed softly. "Runs what's left of the library system. Guardian of dusty wisdom and forgotten truth."

Bully exchanged a glance with Beth and Jackson, then stepped forward. "We're grateful," he said. "Really. We've had a week straight of running, and that fire smells like salvation."

He hesitated, then slowly unburdened the story. "It started with a coin. One I found. Or maybe one that found us. Since then, it's been one long tunnel beneath the earth, a vehicle made of gel, gravity arcs and technology we don't even understand. We traveled under the skin of the world, and when we woke up, we were here."

"And this," he added, tapping the side of his head, "is Chief Red Herringbone MD. We're connected to him. All three of us. Mentally, visually. He's not here, but we see him. He sees us. Talks to us. It's strange, yeah but it's real."

Jackson gave a wry shrug. "Feels like we have a second in command within our own brains most of the time."

Beth nodded, resting her hands near the fire. "But somehow it all feels like it's only just beginning and kind of like we have always been this way but that is not true."

Yoshiko said nothing at first. Just watched them. The way they sat. The way they breathed. The way they moved like kids but carried shadows behind their eyes. Then she looked to her father, who gave a knowing grunt and skewered another strip of meat.

"Well," she finally said, "you're either the strangest liars I've ever met... or something big is about to stir."

And with that, the flames crackled, and the circle of trust widened just a little.

5

"Swift as the wind. Quiet as the forest. Conquer like the fire. Steady as the mountain." Sun Tzu

Bully sat just outside the edge of the firelight, the embers casting soft shadows across the dusty boots he still hadn't gotten used to wearing. Jackson snored lightly somewhere behind him, and Beth stretched out in silence, eyes turned toward the dark swell of the sky. The stars overhead shimmered like scattered circuitry.

But Bully's mind was elsewhere. Inward.

There, in the quiet of his thoughts, he found the thread. The link. The space where Chief Red Herringbone lived not as a voice in his ear, but as a presence just behind the eyes. They didn't need to speak aloud anymore. Bully had discovered something curious: he could aim a thought privately to Red or release it into the shared thread with Beth and Jackson, or keep it tucked inside, his own secret chamber. This was communication redefined quiet, efficient, intimate.

Why the obsidian stone, Chief? he asked silently, casting the thought like a pebble into still water. Why buried treasure at all?

The reply came not in words, at first, but in feeling bittersweet nostalgia wrapped in warmth.

Then, Red's voice followed like a soft breeze through memory.

"Back in 1994, there was a film I loved. All the actors had died by the time I watched it. It was a quiet film. A man named Red leads us to the end of a hard story a hard life. He walks along a stone wall and finds a tree where lovers might sit and there he found a box buried beneath a black obsidian stone. Something left for him by a friend. A promise kept."

Bully pictured it—walking along in tall grass, finding the tree, seeing the glint of the stone.

"It stuck with me," Red continued. "That simple idea that someone, somewhere, might leave hope behind like a breadcrumb. That if someone found it, they could finish what the last one started. I buried that coin like that. Like the stone. Maybe nobody would find it. Maybe nobody would believe it. But maybe just maybe someone like you would." The actor was Morgan Freeman, and his voice echoes his freedom, as he plays Red, "I find I'm so excited I can barely sit still or hold a thought in my head. I think it is the excitement only a free man can feel a free man at the start of a long journey whose conclusion is uncertain."

Bully felt his chest relax, and he grew to appreciate the moment of discovery, but with understanding and at being discovered. He wasn't just a passenger on this journey. He was part of a lineage. A legacy of unfinished dreams.

Thanks, he thought quietly, the firelight flickering across his face. Guess we'd better not waste it.

Chief Red didn't reply. But the warmth that settled into Bully's chest said more than words ever could.

6

"Victory comes from finding opportunities in problems." Sun Tzu

Wade Castle watched as the diggers arrived at Spirit Mound massive machines built for conquest, not delicacy. Their engines growled, belching dust as they inched closer to the sacred earth. But then, one by one, they stuttered. Stalled. Dead. Not for lack of fuel or faulty design something unseen had intervened.

Chief Red Herringbone's security protocols had held. Invisible countermeasures embedded deep in the soil itself. Spirit Mound would not be desecrated without consequence.

Castle didn't curse. He didn't shout. Emotion wasn't in his architecture. Instead, he pivoted cold and efficient. If boots and blades wouldn't penetrate the ground, he'd pierce it from above.

He rerouted orbital satellites, activated dormant imaging tech, and engaged multi-spectrum scans, including experimental X-ray projection systems intended for deep Earth analysis. Layer by layer, the ground peeled back under surveillance stone, sediment, memory. Until something revealed itself.

An arc.

A tunnel of impossible geometry, stretching from the roots of Spirit Mound westward, buried so deep and old it whispered another time. It arced across Dakota stone and silence, terminating near a tributary in Belle Fourche long forgotten, yet humming faintly now with reactivation.

Castle didn't blink, but others did. The telemetry alone shocked GoG's command node. Unknown energy signatures. Unaccounted movements. Unauthorized hope.

The conclusion was immediate.

Full asset deployment authorized.

Every drone in the western territories was rerouted. AI surveillance gridlines snapped into place. Military-grade augments were mobilized. Wade Castle was given unrestricted authority.

The pursuit was no longer local.

It was a war to reclaim silence.

Unbeknownst to Wade Castle and the ever-watchful eyes of the Government of Gold, another figure had been tracking the tremors of resistance quietly, methodically from a perch no drone dared reach.

High atop Black Elk Peak, the highest point between the Rockies and the Pyrenees, a solitary observer had made his camp among windswept rocks and pine-flecked silence. The path he'd climbed wasn't on any map he'd made himself, step by step, through muscle, instinct, and a refusal to be followed.

His name was Raif Artemonov. Ukrainian by blood, possibly Russian depending on who was asking or who was hunting. He spoke little but carried a thick Eastern accent passed down like a relic through generations. His family had perished when he was a child, in a rebel-crushed valley far from the charred center of power, and he'd survived by turning grief into brilliance.

Even then, before he could vote or shave, Raif could decipher military encryption like it was children's poetry. He could rebuild broken radios from rusted coils and map terrain by smell. A savant in the truest sense: no formal training, just raw cognition, sharpened by necessity.

By now, he was legend in certain corners of the dark web. A ghost with a knack for slipping into back channels, decoding chatter that was meant to stay buried. He'd heard the whispers about Spirit Mound before the GoG activated their full resource protocols. He'd seen energy readings the state missed. He'd tracked the gravitational anomaly to a thread of movement stretching from sacred ground to Belle Fourche.

And when he saw the pattern unfold three signals moving too fast, too purposefully to be random something inside him tightened.

He didn't know their names. Didn't know what they'd become. But he knew the system wanted them erased. And he knew that meant they mattered.

He slung his custom optics back over his shoulder, tucked the cracked tablet into his pack, and scanned the horizon once more. The air smelled like a hot summer day and static.

Raif Artemonov didn't work for anyone. But this time, he had a mission. And he would find the teens. Before Castle did.

7

"Be extremely subtle even to the point of formlessness. Be extremely mysterious even to the point of soundlessness." Sun Tzu

At Chief Red's subtle prompting, Bully, Beth, and Jackson revealed the tiny mark just behind their ears a faint pinprick, nearly invisible, where their minds were linked through the neural architecture of the helmet. The connection wasn't just communication. It was a bond. A lattice of shared awareness threaded through consciousness like silk through cloth.

"You don't have to," Bully said, his voice quiet, respectful. "But we'd like you with us. As part of the team."

Yoshiko looked at them, these strangers with perfect skin and strange clothes, who spoke to an invisible mentor and traveled through earth like myth.

She turned to Skinny, standing steady near the fire, arms folded. "What do you think, Pops?"

Skinny scratched his beard, squinting up at the stars. "This ain't my road to walk, Yo. But if your heart's pointed that way, you should ride it. No one else gets to steer your saddle."

Yo didn't hesitate.

With a breath, she removed her hat and stepped forward, cradling the helmet in both hands. The others watched in silence as she raised it overhead. The device responded instantly unfolding like a blooming metal flower, welcoming her head with eerie precision. It sealed around her skull with a soft whir.

Then just as with the others a whisper of pressure, a pinprick.

"What" she murmured, blinking.

On the projection before them, the coyote flickered, shimmered then reformed into the now-familiar face of Chief Red Herringbone, MD.

He smiled softly. "Hello, Yoshiko. Fourth time's the charm."

Only she could hear his voice now, threading into her thoughts, gentle but curious.

"Tell me what do you know of your past? Your name. Your blood. Where you came from."

"I don't," she replied inwardly. "Just that I was left behind. I've always felt different."

Red paused, then asked carefully, "May I run a test? A quick blood draw. I believe you may be related to someone I once knew one of my closest friends."

She gave the barest nod inside the helmet.

A light flickered at her temple. A second, gentler pinprick.

"Ouch," she muttered, then chuckled. "Actually... that barely tickled."

The analysis began in silence.

And while she sat among her new companions, her heart thudded not with fear, but with the strange certainty of someone beginning to remember something they hadn't yet known.

In the world that once was, DNA results could take months. But beneath the helmet threaded to technology lost to most of civilization the process took seconds. As the strands aligned and the profile resolved, Chief Red Herringbone's voice filled Yo's mind with measured certainty.

"Your great-great-grandfather was a Mars Pilot," he said. "Japanese-born. Worked with NASA and Roscosmos during the final days of joint interplanetary exploration. His name was Koichi Nakamura but to those who knew him best, he was Sensei Koi. Ninth-degree black belt in the old ways, master of both movement and mind. One of my closest friends."

There was reverence in his tone. Something unshakable.

"To discover that you carry his DNA," Red continued, "is... incredible. I can't tell you what it means to know that a piece of him survived. That you survived."

Then, a pause. A memory resurfaced.

"Before I died," he added, quieter now, "I gave Koi something. A gift box. Something meant for the future. I don't know if it was ever opened but I hoped that one day someone like you would find it. Because it's part of this story now. Your story."

Yo's breath caught not in fear, but recognition.

There is a box.

A strange, beautifully crafted container tucked away in the dim back corners of the old library, shelved like an enigma. She'd dusted it off more times than she could count, always curious, always stymied by its lack of visible lock or keyhole. Just a box that felt unfinished. Waiting.

In that moment, her past and future snapped into alignment like the final page of a long-forgotten book.

She turned her eyes toward the shadowed skyline of Belle Fourche, heart quickening.

"I think I know where it is," she whispered.

And the others leaned in, the firelight flickering like destiny on the verge.

Yo slid the helmet off slowly, her fingers lingering on its smooth edge. The moment it cleared her head, something shifted. Her vision shimmered just slightly then settled. And then she saw him.

Chief Red Herringbone, MD.

Not in the flesh, but in her periphery, in the air beside her like a softly glowing specter. His voice threaded into her hearing as seamlessly as it had for the others.

Jackson was the first to speak, still blinking through the wonder of his post-transformation clarity. "Can I ask you something? About the gel the breathable liquid we were floating in I feel healthier than I've ever felt in my life. Stronger. Like I am clean inside."

Chief Red chuckled gently. "A fair question. "You're not wrong, Jackson. That substance—what you call the gel—was inspired in part by science fiction. Books, old films, far-fetched dreams. One in particular, The Abyss, from 1989—used a concept like it. A liquid that could be breathed. At the time, fantasy. But over decades, with the right chemistry, persistence, and just enough desperation... we made it real."

Beth raised an eyebrow. "So, we really breathed that stuff?"

Red nodded. "You did. And what you breathed wasn't just oxygen in another form, it was a molecular bridge. It carried adaptive compounds designed to change the way your body deals with trauma, pressure, even age."

Yo glanced sideways, uncertain. "So, I'll have to breathe this gel too?"

"Yes," Red said, his tone warm but clear. "You won't drown. But you also won't remember it, not consciously. The first time, your body panics until it learns. Once your cells adapt to breathing in two mediums, you'll be capable of more than you think."

He paused. Then came the part he always delivered with both pride and gravity.

"Koi and I your great-great-grandfather we pioneered something together. A fusion of human DNA with the resilience of one of nature's most indestructible creatures: the tardigrade. It lives through radiation, vacuum, extremes no life should endure. We took its essence and made it human-compatible."

His gaze softened.

"That fusion now lives in you. It means longer life. Faster recovery. And a body more suited to the world that's coming."

Yo looked down at her hands, flexing her fingers as though seeing them for the first time.

Bully leaned forward, smiling. "Welcome to the team."

He paused. Then came the part he always delivered with both pride and gravity.

His gaze softened.

Yoshiko glanced at the others Bully, Beth, Jackson each radiating strength and vitality that hadn't been there days before. Whatever they had endured, it had changed them. And they were alive. Alive and well.

A slow smile touched the corners of her mouth.

"If they came out of it looking like this," she said, brushing a loose strand of hair from her cheek, "then I'm willing to try it too. Just… maybe not today."

Chief Red chuckled in her mind, the sound warm and approving.

But before they could speak more of breath-gel and biological transformation, Yo's thoughts turned to something else something older.

"The box," she murmured, eyes narrowing slightly. "The Himitsu-Bako."

She stood and dusted off her jeans. "Before anything else, we need to open it."

She led them into the dim heart of the crumbling library. There, amidst forgotten shelves and sun-faded posters, nestled beneath a thick veil of dust and time, rested the box carved from ancient wood, its surface etched with an intricate maze of sliding panels.

"I never figured it out," Yo admitted. "The box doesn't have a lock or key, just layers. My father said it came from my great-great-grandfather's belongings. Said it was important. But I didn't understand why until now."

Chief Red's voice returned, quieter now, reverent.

"It's a Japanese Himitsu-Bako. A secret box. Crafted not to guard treasure, but to guard truth. And this one was solved only once, by Sergei my friend, your ancestor's ally. He left something inside. Something meant for you."

Beth crouched beside it, tracing the polished wood with a fingertip. "It's beautiful," she whispered.

Red's voice cut back in, solemn and firm.

"It will take one hundred precise movements to unlock. No more, no less. No brute force. No shortcuts. Only memory. Patience. And the will to know."

The room fell silent.

And in that silence, the past leaned forward waiting to be remembered.

8

"Tactics without strategy is the noise before defeat."
Sun Tzu

The six of them, Bully, Beth, Jackson, Yoshiko, Skinny, and the ever-present shimmer of Chief Red in their shared vision moved low through the brittle grass and shadow. The sky above buzzed with tension: a swarm of drones thousands slicing patterns across the moonlit clouds like mechanical vultures.

The six of them ducked behind a gnarled hulk of an old cottonwood, now grown wild and wreathed in prairie brush. From there, they could hear the distant rhythm of boots on cracked pavement. Infantry. Marching with slow, deliberate cadence. Not scouts enforcers. And at the rear, unmistakable and terrible in his stillness, strode Wade Castle. A blunt instrument in human form. His armor didn't gleam. It absorbed light.

The Government of Gold hadn't found them yet.

But they were too close.

When the boots passed and the whine of drones faded into the sweep of wind, the six broke from cover and dashed toward the skeletal outline of the library. The entrance hissed slightly as they slipped through, one after the other, the old security doors still responsive to Chief Red's biometric echo.

Inside, silence.

But just as the final latch clicked behind them, a seventh presence coasted in silently.

The figure moved like vapor, balanced atop a single, motorized wheel matte black unicycle powered by nothing louder than thought. Wrapped in a mesh of adaptive camouflage that flickered faintly as it disengaged, the stranger rolled to a stop near the dimly lit stacks.

Everyone froze.

Skinny half-reached for his knife. Bully's eyes narrowed. Even Yoshiko stepped instinctively between the intruder and the ancient box they had come to unlock.

The figure dismounted with fluid precision, pulled back a hood stitched with optical fibers and revealed a sharp, solemn face beneath.

"I followed the arc," he said, Eastern European accent clinging to each word like frost. "And I followed the signal you lit when you stepped out of the earth."

He looked to the teens' faces unreadable, voice low and certain.

"My name is Raif Artemonov," he said slow and deliberate, stepping fully into the dim light on the library entrance. "My friends call me Ralph—it's easier on the ears."

He scanned each of their faces, voice low but steady. "I know you don't know me. But I've been watching the signals, the movement, the silence around you and silence like that only follows something important."

A pause, then the truth at his core.

"I'm with the rebellion whatever that is and I hope that you are. Or what is left of it. I didn't come to spy, or to lead. I came because you're being hunted by something that doesn't lose. And I don't believe in letting kids get erased without a fight. I think I am also about the same age as all of you."

He slipped off his glove, extended a hand calloused, firm, real.

"I'm here to protect you. If you'll let me."

The library's walls groaned with age as the team of four soon to be five tucked the intricate puzzle box and the helmet into the backpack. Every second counted now.

Ralph, seated cross-legged near the back wall beneath a half-lit exit sign, cracked open his battered laptop. The keys of the laptop were worn to smooth stone, but his hands danced across them with quiet precision. A second later, the feed from Chief Red Herringbone MD blinked to life on-screen.

Chief Red raised an eyebrow. "Impressive," he said. "Clean entry. Minimal noise. Ralph, you're a ghost with a keyboard."

Ralph gave a modest nod. "I'm better with silence than words."

Red's expression shifted. Focused. "Then let's give them a trail of noise."

He straightened, the glint of urgency cutting through his usual calm. "It's time to live up to the name: Red Herring. We're going to manufacture a deception big enough to divert GoG's full attention and I know exactly how."

He turned toward Skinny, who stood by the broken doorway tightening the worn leather straps of his saddlebags under his arm against his body.

Chief Red, said to Skinny "I need a spectacle. Something that looks like the teens are heading for a high-tech relic cache buried in the backside of Mount Rushmore an ancient resistance vault that doesn't exist. We'll scatter bio-cloaked signal decoys and generate a heat trail using drone carcasses and clothing scraps soaked with their visual profile. If they scan it, they'll think our team went up and into the hills. That'll buy us three, maybe four hours."

Skinny met his gaze. "And you want me to ride up front."

Red nodded solemnly. "Ride hard. Fast. Make sure they see someone alive, someone that fits the silhouette of the boy. Burn every breadcrumb you drop. We'll feed them the decoy trail from here. But they'll give chase once the scent hits."

A silence passed.

Then Skinny, weathered and wiry, let out a short laugh. "I reckon my old bones remember how to make a little noise." He looked to Yo. "If it buys you time, girl, then I'd ride through fire for it."

Beth whispered, "Won't they realize the trick?"

Red smiled faintly. "Eventually. But by then, we'll be in the sky, chasing what's real."

He turned serious again. "Remember don't crush the puzzle box. I heard Jackson and Bully talking about it. If you damage it, the internal mechanism self-destructs, and with it, the key to the treasure's next phase. You'll need all five of you to solve it. It requires pattern memory, spatial perception, and instinctive timing. I estimate three hours to unlock it and that's with full focus."

He looked to the group. "Once that's done, you'll need to use the two keys both coin keys to unlock the top portion with all the words the top will spin direction and another hidden door around the base will open with the third key. After that, we'll head west fast. There's a hidden hanger outside Belle Fourche. A pre-collapse prop plane, fueled, retrofitted. Destination: Ludlow."

He looked directly at Skinny.

"This ruse it only works if they believe it. Are you ready to risk everything?"

Skinny put the saddle on his horse, swung a leg over the saddle, reins loose in his hands. On the back of the horse a transponder to make the horse look like three horses.

"For her?" he said, tipping his chin toward Yo. "Always. I love you, Missy"

And with that, Skinny vanished into dusk and an echo in motion, a flame in the wind, a red herring riding into legend.

At first, Wade Castle didn't hear the distant thunder of hooves just the whisper of dust on stone and the ticking readout of drone telemetry. He was scanning the tracks hoofprints, dry and deliberate etched into the fractured earth like punctuation from an earlier age. Horses. Old-world, low-tech, faster over this terrain than anything he had on foot.

Castle's gaze narrowed. Infantry was too slow, too noisy, too hard footed for this kind of terrain. With the precision of someone who didn't waste energy on blame, he issued a flat directive:

"Disband the ground line. Deploy mobile cavalry assets. Class Three Riders. Silent frames. Infrared tracking."

Within the hour, GoG's infantry columns were rerouted exiting the canyon floor like a flood reversing course. In their place came something leaner. Sleeker. Rough Riders.

Drone horses, engineered for terrain and terror, glided in low to the ground. Their hooves made no sound. Their armored torsos shimmered in the infrared haze, and each was manned by riders bred for efficiency: minimal conversation, maximum elimination. Armed with neural-synced rifles and pursuit algorithms, they needed only a whisper of signal.

Two hours passed. Then came the ping, the movement of Skinny Colley racing into the mountains on passes working his way toward the presidents faces.

A faint but distinct trace three figures, horseback, cutting fast through the canyons east of Mount Rushmore. High body heat. Irregular movement. No engine trace.

Castle's eyes didn't widen. But something in his posture tightened. "They're running," he said quietly. "Which means they're hiding something."

He mounted his own steed—part machine, part storm—and gave the command. "Full pursuit. Eyes sharp. Guns hot. Until I say otherwise."

And like that, the chase began in earnest across dry ridges, shadowed valleys, and the long-forgotten spine of a monument carved in a time that no longer ruled the world.

While the others huddled around the puzzle box, its lacquered panels clicking softly in the quiet the atmosphere inside the old library shifted. There was a sense of gravity, of something quietly momentous unfolding beneath the dust and flickering lights.

Chief Red's presence lit the air beside them, his voice as composed as ever. "Ralph," he said, "you've proven yourself more than capable in the shadows. Would you like to be part of this team, formally? Added to the neural catalogue?"

Ralph didn't answer right away. His eyes drifted to the others shoulders hunched over the Himitsu-Bako, lips moving silently as they coordinated through thought. Together. Not alone. That word meant something.

"I would," he said simply.

9

The Supreme art of war is to subdue the enemy without fighting." Sun Tzu

Red gave a nod. "Bully, the helmet, if you please."

Bully handed it over without a word. Ralph held the weight of it in his hands, studying the curve, the precision. Then, with a quiet breath, he lowered it over his head.

Just like before, the helmet responded opening gently, wrapping itself around his skull with surgical elegance. A moment later, a pinprick of light. The neural thread locked in.

"You may feel a slight" Red began.

"I don't," Ralph said, voice calm. "Not compared to what I've felt in the past."

His perception expanded. Visual overlays shimmered into view. Information flared behind his eyes. The crude AI systems he'd rigged together from scavenged parts paled in comparison. This upgrade threaded into his very cognition faster, cleaner, predictive. His reach into GoG networks would now be surgical.

For the first time in a long time, Ralph didn't feel like an outsider staring through the glass. He was part of something. Finally.

Red's tone softened. "One more thing. May I analyze your DNA? Just a quick sample. I have reason to believe you carry legacy in your blood."

Ralph offered his hand without hesitation. "You'll find it," he said.

Red did. The sample confirmed it moments later.

"Your great-great-grandfather," Red said, "was a Roscosmos Mars Lander Pilot. One of the most brilliant men I've ever known. I remember him precise, intuitive, a statistical savant who could forecast failure before it even began."

Ralph gave a faint smile. "Those were the stories. I'm just the last one left to remember them."

Red's image shimmered with pride. "Not anymore."

For two straight hours, the team wrestled with the box not in anger, but in mounting waves of frustration. The Himitsu-Bako remained stubbornly elegant, offering nothing but smooth surfaces and silent resistance. The key was inside. They all felt it. But finding the delicate sheath of movement one tiny shift among a hundred false starts was maddening.

Somewhere in the middle of it, morale dipped.

That's when Yo quietly produced a dusty stash from her canvas satchel metal cans of something like spiced meat, their labels flaking but still legible only the name of it was missing, relics of a century-old culinary gamble and quite famous. Preserved beyond reason, the meat hissed faintly as it hit the old skillet they'd repurposed. It wasn't gourmet. But under the weight of exhaustion and adrenaline, it tasted like memory and resolve.

Fed and warmed, Bully was the first to return to the task. He slid one panel carefully, slowly as far as it would go.

A soft click.

He looked up, surprised. "There."

Jackson took the box next. His fingers found a recessed panel just beside the one Bully had moved. Another shift. Another click.

Beth stepped in and, with a strange rhythm like tapping a melody only she could hear, coaxed out five more sliding segments clicks building like a drumroll. Her grin said she didn't entirely know how she'd done it.

Then Yo, lit by something fierce, found ten in rapid succession. Her breath caught, her hands flying with certainty.

And finally, Ralph stepped forward. His eyes didn't blink. His fingers moved as though tracing an equation only he could see. With cold precision, he made the final rotations each deliberate, each exact.

The box sighed open.

Inside, nestled in velvet and silence, lay the coin key. An identical twin to the one Bully carried etched with symbols that four understood and soon six would fully know, gleaming faintly like it knew it had been found.

Red's voice echoed with quiet satisfaction: "Three hours. Right on time."

With reverence, Beth closed the box. Yo gently replaced the helmet beside it. Ralph sealed the backpack, tightening the straps. And Bully, without a word, accepted the new coin fingers curling around it like it had always belonged to him.

Whatever came next, they were ready.

The lock was open. And the world had shifted.

10

"The greatest victory is that which requires no battle."
Sun Tzu

Skinny Colley was born of wild country; a man etched from dust and determination. He could ride up hills like the wind had given him instructions, saddle deep in instinct and grit. His horse moved like an extension of his will, no hesitation, no waste.

As the sound of drones swelled behind him like a swarm of angry wasps, Skinny stayed focused. He rode hard, slipping through narrow canyon passes and zigzagging trails, always just out of reach. He moved like a ghost from another time until the drones got too close.

He didn't flinch.

From the saddle, he drew his antique rifle one he'd refurbished himself and with the poise of a man who'd been shooting on horseback since boyhood, took three drones clean out of the sky. Pop. Pop. Pop. Sparks bloomed behind him like fireworks made of violence.

But Wade Castle had already drawn his rifle. He didn't hesitate. He never did.

One shot.

Skinny dropped like a fallen flag, his body curling around the saddle as his horse galloped at a few more paces before stopping, confused by the sudden stillness.

Back atop Mount Rushmore, Castle pressed forward, unaware of what had been gained by what had been lost. The drones swarmed the ridgeline. Castle and his elite climbed toward the shadowed cave behind the chiseled faces of long-dead presidents, driven by a purpose colder than honor.

Miles away, in the faded hush of Belle Fourche's forgotten halls, Chief Red felt it. The loss flickered like static through the neural net, and his voice came through the link not loud, not broken, just soft.

"Yoshiko I'm sorry. Skinny's gone."

The team fell into silence. Tears and lots of hugs.

They sat among shattered chairs and collapsed shelves, the Himitsu-Bako still warm from their hands. No one spoke. No one needed to. They embraced quietly, tears slipping down cheeks streaked with effort and resolve. They cried for a mountain man who had given everything. For a father who wasn't bound by blood, but by choice.

They would mourn properly later.

11

"Engage people with what they respect; it is what they are able to discern and confirms their projections. While you wait for the extraordinary moment."
Sun Tzu

Because right now, they were climbing again this time, the worn stairs of the Center of the Nation monument. The wind hissed through the narrow cracks in the stone, and at the summit, flanked by the metal bones of the old steel center, Bully halted.

Set into the topmost foot wide piece of metal on the platform, right where the heart of the country was meant to beat, were two indentations perfectly round, etched with ancient precision.

He reached for the coin keys.

Destiny waited.

Bully crouched at the top cylinder of the Center of the Nation monument, the two coin keys held tightly in his hands. He fit them into the twin indents, one on the one side facing north and one on the other side facing south a perfect circle etched with time-worn precision.

He exhaled. Try to turn them. They wouldn't budge. Not alone. "Jackson," he called quietly. "I need you."

Without hesitation, Jackson stepped forward, boots echoing softly against the stone. They locked their eyes. And together, hands braced on the cool metal, they counted.

"One. Two, Three."

The keys turned with a deep, resonant clunk, it was both a metallic sound and stone sound of movement. Mechanisms groaned inside the monument like tectonic plates shifting. Then a portion of the stonework at the base trembled and slowly, a door began to open.

The slab sank backward, then slid aside, revealing a dark chamber no one had seen in generations.

Inside, nestled on a raised platform beneath beams of flickering light, lay a key unlike the others.

Slim. Heavy. Made of aged titanium alloy. Its grip was ribbed like a missile's tail, and its notched head bore one unmistakable design: the launch interface of a Cold War-era nuclear warhead.

Bully stared. Beth whispered, "What is that?"

"A kingdom can't be restored without power," Red replied. "This key is part of that process. But it isn't enough on its own. There's a few more treasures one more piece of the old world which is better tech that anything that I have seen so far and that which will help you find the four quarters of a dream catcher and you need to find before the real building begins."

Yo looked down at the strange artifact, her voice steadier than she expected. "Where do we go next?"

Red paused. The wind brushed across the hills below them like breath held too long.

"Ludlow, Harding County, North."

Under the hush of night, the six made their way up the broken road Bully, Beth, Jackson, Yo, and Ralph plus in the periphery Chief Red, shadows long beneath starlight.

The old Belle Fourche airfield loomed ahead, silent and forgotten its hangar doors flanked by rusted fencing and overgrowth, as if time had tried to seal it off. But Chief Red had kept it hidden in plain sight, purchased and protected long before they were born. A quiet contingency.

The teens trailed in a loose pack, the way young people walk when they are tired or bored. They were tired. Hungry again. And whining in whispers that barely disguised the fear underneath.

"Do we have to walk this far?" Jackson muttered.

"Why's the road always uphill?" Beth added.

"I think my spleen is bruised," Bully sighed, dragging his feet with theatrical flair.

Ralph, oldest by maybe a year but aged by a lifetime of solitude, simply walked. His silence was steady.

Chief Red appeared just ahead of them, his projection flickering slightly as he was standing still in their minds eye, overlaid against the weeds and cracked tarmac. His voice came calm, even warm.

"You're all between fifteen and seventeen old enough to know burden, but young enough to still carry it with hope. That's rare. And powerful."

He paused.

"Bill Gates a visionary technologist, philanthropist, and global influencer once said, 'I believe that if you show people the problems and you show them solutions they will be moved to act.' That's what I've tried to do with each of you. And as Sun Tzu reminded us a millennia ago: 'He will win who knows when to fight and when not to fight."

He turned his gaze to Yoshiko, who stared ahead with fierce resolve, jaw tight.

"Yo, I know your heart burns for justice. For your father. For what was taken from you. But your strength, like all strength, must be guided. Right now, the mission is not vengeance, it's survival. It's growth. This moment is for learning how to fight. With intelligence. With unity. With the unique gifts each of you carry."

Beth stared at Chief Red and said, "sometimes the best thing to say is nothing." And she gave Yo her hand to hold as they continued to walk.

They reached the hangar gate. A retinal scanner blinked to life and accepted Red's imprint with a click using Bully's eyes, not that is a trick. The heavy doors creaked open to reveal the darkened hulk of a fixed-wing prop plane pre-collapse tech, retrofitted and waiting.

As the hangar door sighed open and light spilled into the sealed chamber, the team stepped inside, their eyes adjusting to the glow. Then, with a low hum, the interior lights flickered to life. Somewhere within the framework of the ceiling, ancient sensors awoke—flickering, then stabilizing—recognizing the presence they had waited generations to greet.

12

"Know yourself and you will win all battles." Sun Tzu

From a projection node above the cockpit, a spectral figure materialized shimmering, not ethereal, but exact, solid in presence and spirit. The warrior stood tall, eyes fierce beneath a feathered helm, wrapped in regalia that shifted subtly in the light. His voice cut like flint.

"Stay back!" The command echoed in Lakota, his tone thunderous with purpose. "This place is sacred. Not yours!"

The five teens froze, their instincts pulling taut. But Chief Red stepped forward, unafraid.

Then, with reverence in his voice, he returned the greeting not just with words, but with the cadence and spirit of the old ways. The phrases were simple, the gesture ancient: a recognition of kinship, of shared earth and vision.

The warrior blinked, and his form softened. The spear of suspicion gave way to the open hand of welcome.

"Red." His tone was different now worn with warmth, the way an old guardian might address a younger flame. "You came after all. And you brought them."

The figure identified himself: Chief Old Horse, digital sentinel, spiritual anchor. A leader of tribes bound by blood, but also by memory and purpose. He had watched the skies, logged the trespassers curious, lost, or predatory but none had carried the signature of Red's blood, or the purpose bound into this mission.

He spoke of the tribes who had held ceremony across the plains long after the cities crumbled, whose quiet strength became the soul of the land. Their messages, stored and encrypted in the AI's core memory, offered greeting blessings of wind, stone, fire, and rain.

Chief Red introduced the five with the quiet pride of a father presenting his children to the ancestors: Bully, kind, protective and full of heart an old soul; Beth, carries the storm and runs always looking to sky; Jackson, strong and able to block others using his core and arms; Yoshiko, precise, alert, a cowgirl and fiercely loyal; and Ralph, the wild card untamed brilliance, master hacker, and tough as nails.

"These are not just survivors," Red said. "They're carriers. Of culture, of story, of tomorrow."

But even in the sacred calm, Red's voice turned shadowed.

"Wade Castle will come. GoG too. This place is not a secret anymore. We'll need time. And you, Chief Old Horse, are its last protector."

The AI warrior nodded slowly. Not as code responding to input, but as one soul acknowledging another.

"Then I stand watch. As I have. As I will. Do you have the million miniature versions of myself they might be helpful". Chief Red blinked into existence the entire group of all the miniature versions of Chief Old Horse which had been at the Spirit Mound and were now present on the floor in the hanger.

Red's voice echoed inside.

"Now, Ralph I have a question for you."

Ralph looked up.

"Do you think you could learn to fly that?"
"With your instinct? Your mathematics? Your sense of systems and rhythm"

Ralph said "I believe you can."

There was a beat of quiet. Then Ralph nodded once.

"I'll learn," he said. "With you guiding me I'll fly it."

And just like that, the night shifted from mourning to mission. The sky wasn't the end it was the next beginning.

This is the End of Chapter Book 2

Coming Soon Thesaurum Intra Chapter Books 3 and 4

"If you know the enemy and know yourself, you need not fear the result of a hundred battles." Sun Tzu

Made in the USA
Coppell, TX
17 January 2026

67256585R10059